Healing the Boss's Heart
Valerie Hansen

Steeple
Hill®

Published by Steeple Hill Books™

Special thanks and acknowledgment to Valerie Hansen
for her contribution to the After the Storm miniseries.

STEEPLE HILL BOOKS

Steeple
Hill®

Recycling programs
for this product may
not exist in your area.

ISBN-13: 978-0-373-81414-5

HEALING THE BOSS'S HEART

www.SteepleHill.com

Printed in U.S.A.

The Lord is good, a refuge in times or trouble.
He cares for those who trust in Him.
—*Nahum* 1:7

Special thanks to the other authors who participated with me in this series, After the Storm: Annie Jones, Brenda Minton, Carolyne Aarsen, Patricia Davids and Kathryn Springer.

Some of us actually live in Tornado Alley, so all those brave folks who have pitched in to restore our neighborhoods after similar disasters are especially dear to our hearts.

Chapter One

"The Lord is good, a refuge in times of trouble. He cares for those who trust in Him."

—Nahum 1:7

July 10, 3:54 p.m.

"Unbelievable," Gregory Garrison muttered under his breath, his mood mirroring the prairie storm that was developing outside his Main Street office.

If there had been an award for Grumpiest Boss of the Month, Maya Logan would have known *exactly* who to nominate. Accepting the position as Mr. Garrison's executive assistant had been a step up in her secretarial career but she was beginning to question her decision to start working for his investment firm, no matter how wonderful the wages. The man was obsessive. And when things didn't go exactly as he'd envisioned, he could be a real bear. Like now.

Turning away to hide her amusement, she busied herself at her desk while her employer paced and continued to mumble to himself.

Tall and broad-shouldered, with hazel eyes and chestnut-brown hair, Gregory Garrison was not only good-looking, as many single women in High Plains had noticed since his recent return, he had the kind of forceful personality that competitors and allies alike admired. It was that same unbending, always-right attitude that was so off-putting to Maya. She'd had her fill of that kind of unreasonable man when…

"*Now* look what he's doing," Gregory said, interrupting her thoughts. He gestured out the plate-glass window at a young boy riding a bicycle in tight, skidding circles.

She looked up. "Oh, that. I thought you were upset over the glitches in the Atkinson merger."

"I was. I am," he said. "But that ill-mannered little troublemaker is driving me crazy. Look, he's trying to splash mud all over my windows."

Her brown eyes twinkled with repressed mirth. "Sure looks like it. Sorry about that."

"Well, what are you going to do?"

"Me? Do?"

"Yes. There wouldn't be any mud on the sidewalk in the first place if you hadn't insisted on bringing in those planters along the walkway."

"I didn't realize they'd overflow if we got too much rain," Maya said. "Relax. Tommy's not hurting anything. He's just a kid."

Gregory was adamant. "He has no business riding that bike all over town, let alone being out in this kind of weather by himself. Why don't his parents look after him?"

She joined her boss in the center of the compact office before answering, "Tommy's parents are dead. He's in foster care with Beth and Brandon Otis."

"Aren't they responsible for him?"

"Yes, but as far as I know, that's already his

third placement and he can't be more than six years old. The poor kid must feel pretty lost. My brothers and I really foundered after our parents were killed, and we weren't children. I was eighteen at the time and my brothers were even older."

"That's still no excuse for allowing him to run loose. If he's this unruly now, what will he be like in his teens?"

Mentally contrasting her wandering brother, Clay, with their other, more stable sibling, Jesse, she said, "Tommy'll be fine. He just needs to sow a few wild oats, or in this case, run through a few puddles. It's hot and muggy out there, so he won't get chilled. And the storm seems to be slacking up. It's no big deal."

"It will be when he throws mud on my building or loses his balance and crashes into the window or a parked car," Gregory insisted.

Just as he finished speaking, thunder boomed in the distance and made Maya jump. "Or gets hit by lightning. Okay. I'll go shoo him away." She raked her slim fingers through her feathery, light brown hair and let it fall back into place naturally.

"Will I have to listen to you moaning about your ruined hairdo if you get rained on?"

"You might." She wanted to add that her short cut was easy enough to dry and style in minutes, but she wanted to make a point. She was a professional business assistant, not Gregory Garrison's servant or gofer.

"Never mind," he said flatly. "I'll send the little pest packing myself." He slipped off his expensively tailored suit jacket and handed it to her without another word.

Smiling in spite of diligent efforts to keep a straight face, Maya watched Greg stride to the door, jerk it open and step out onto the sidewalk.

The rain was now coming down so hard it nearly obscured her view of the park across the street, but Maya could still see her boss through the plate-glass window. Although he was standing fairly close to the building, his blue silk shirt was plastered to him in seconds and looked every bit as wet as the boy's striped T-shirt.

"Serves you right," Maya muttered.

"Imagine that. A grown man picking on a poor little kid."

Her grin widened. If Tommy Jacobs was half as wily and agile as her brother Clay had been at that age, the fastidious Mr. Garrison was in for a big, big surprise. She could hardly wait to see him get his comeuppance.

Greg paused under the carved limestone overhang of his historic building's facade. The wind-driven water found him with a vengeance just the same, making him wish he'd had the foresight to install a wide awning the way many of the other businesses on Main Street had. He should have known he'd need it. He'd grown up in High Plains and had experienced hundreds of similar Kansas storms.

Then again, he mused, disgusted, anybody with a lick of sense would have stayed inside until the rain had stopped for good—mud or no mud.

He shouted and waved to the boy. "Hey! You. Tommy. Come here."

The child slid his bike to a stop on the brick-paved roadway, almost overcorrecting and taking a tumble when his front tire bumped the curb.

It amazed him to see that much athletic prowess in one so young. Maybe the boy was older than Maya thought and merely small for his age.

Moderating his tone, Greg tried again. He didn't know a lot about boys, other than having been one himself. "I just want to talk to you for a second, Tommy. Come here. Please?"

The freckle-faced boy shook his head, sending droplets flying from his hair and the end of his little nose. "No way, Mister."

"Don't make me come over there and get you," Greg warned. "All I want to do is talk. Honest."

"My dog'll bite you if you touch me," Tommy replied. "Charlie takes care of me."

For the first time, Greg noticed a medium-sized, black-and-white mongrel standing beside the boy. That poor dog looked even more soaked than Tommy. If the dog weren't panting and looking extremely pleased with its current adventure, he'd have assumed it was suffering.

"I'm not going to hurt you," Greg assured

Tommy. "I just wanted to ask you why you were trying to mess up my building?"

"I dunno. 'Cause it's fun?"

"Not for me, it isn't."

"Oh."

"Is that all you have to say for yourself?"

"Guess so." He straightened the handlebars, put one foot on a pedal and leaned to the side, obviously getting ready to ride off.

"Wait," Greg said, eyeing the blackening sky and recalling similar unsettled weather conditions from his own childhood. "How far is it to your house?"

"I don't have a house. I'm an orphan." The boy's words were clipped, angry-sounding.

"I mean the place where you live right now."

"None of your business." Tommy winced as the first bits of hail began to pelt him. "Ouch!"

"Get in here under cover," Greg shouted, realizing the danger. "That stuff can get big enough to knock out a full grown cow."

Ignoring him, Tommy dropped his bike and began swatting uselessly at the pellets of ice that were now falling in far greater numbers. "Ow, ow, ow!"

At the end of his patience, Greg took four long strides and made a grab for Tommy while he was distracted. The wind had picked up and was driving the already nickel-size chunks of hail at them with stinging force. There was no more time to argue.

A siren began to wail. Bending against the wind and struggling to stay on his feet, Greg hunched over the boy to shield him and glanced down Main Street where a distant police car had begun flashing its red-and-blue lights.

Townspeople were scattering right and left. Umbrellas were turning inside out with a quick snap, making them worse than useless. Passersby had pulled jackets and whatever else they had at hand over their heads and were scrambling for cover. In the park across the street, a mother grabbed her toddler and made a wild dash for safety, abandoning his plastic-canopied stroller and the rest of her belongings to the storm.

Trash cans along the street and in the park

toppled with a bang and dumped their contents. Some rolled in tight arcs, kept from blowing away by the slim chains that held them to their stanchions, while others tore loose and tumbled toward the High Plains River to the north.

This newer, more powerful wind carried strange odors, as if a freshly plowed field suddenly had become airborne. There was grass and cedar and ozone in the mix, too. That meant the weather was about to become even more perilous.

Freezing for only an instant, Greg strained to listen. Every sense was alert. His pulse was pounding in his ears so loudly he wasn't sure what he was actually hearing. A dull humming echoed in the distance, then increased in volume.

Frightening memories came flooding back, fears that he had kept buried since childhood.

How could this be happening? The morning had been warm. Balmy. There had been no tornado watches or warnings in effect that he knew of, nor had there been a peep out of the town's antiquated alarm system.

That didn't matter now. The hum had grown to a roar and seemed to be coming from the southwest. Unless he was imagining things, High Plains was about to be hit by a twister!

Greg pivoted and peered into the sheeting rain and ice crystals, trying to make out anything definitive. It was hopeless. All he could see was blackness in the distance and a gray pall overhead.

Wind-driven hail had punched holes in the bright red-and-white awning over the front of Elmira's Pie Shop next door. The canvas was whipping so violently it was beginning to shred and tear away from its frame. Other bits of material were blowing past, too, some large enough to do serious damage to anything or anyone in the way.

"Come on, kid. I'm done arguing," he shouted, staying bent over and slinging the small child into his arms.

The boy struggled. His loose bicycle went skidding across the pavement and on down the brick street as if it were weightless.

Shrieking, "Charlie!" Tommy reached toward the place where his dog had been.

Instead of staying with him, the mutt had tucked its tail and was headed for the park across the street.

He was frantic. "Charlie!"

Greg ducked into the safety of the office door archway just as the police car finally reached them and cruised past, its occupant broadcasting a "take cover" order over the sound of the wailing, pulsing siren.

Tommy was kicking and pounding on him with his tight little fists. "No! I have to get Charlie!"

Struggling to stay balanced while holding the child, Greg paused in the doorway. Using its protruding stone frame as a temporary shelter, he took one last look at the menacing sky.

There was no doubt about it. He couldn't spot a funnel cloud yet but he was positive trouble was coming—with a vengeance. Straight-line winds were already causing plenty of havoc and a tornado would probably finish the job.

Lush cottonwood trees across the street bent and thrashed about as if they were about to be ripped to shreds. Many small branches and leaves had already torn loose and were flying away like tattered green confetti.

A few foolish people had taken to their cars, apparently hoping to outrun the storm, and were now reduced to peering through shattered and pocked windshields as they crept along the street in newly dented vehicles. At least the cars' windshields were made of safety glass and didn't completely fall apart when they were hit. If those cars didn't end up airborne, their occupants would probably be okay. If a twister caught and lifted them, however, they would be in serious, possibly deadly, trouble.

During the years he'd spent up north, Greg had forgotten how terrifying the forces of nature could be in the plains. Unfortunately, it was all coming back to him. Vividly.

Maya had been watching with growing concern and already had her car keys in hand when she jerked open the door to admit her boss and Tommy. "Get inside. Quick!"

He thrust the squirming child at her. "Here. Take him. I'm going back after his dog."

"Don't be ridiculous." She clutched his arm and pointed. "You'll never catch it. Look."

Debris was swirling through the air in ever-increasing amounts and the hail had begun to pile in lumpy drifts along the curb. It had flattened the flowers she'd so lovingly placed in the planters and buried their stubbly remnants under inches of white, icy crystals.

In the distance, Tommy's dog was disappearing into the maelstrom. Unless the frightened animal responded to commands to return, there was no chance of anyone catching up to it.

Gregory took a deep breath and hollered, "Charlie," but Maya could tell he was wasting his breath. The soggy mongrel didn't even slow.

"Take the boy and head for the basement," Gregory yelled at her. Ducking inside, he had to put his shoulder to the heavy door and use his full weight to close and latch it.

She shoved Tommy back at him. "No. I have to go get Layla."

"In this weather? Don't be an idiot."

"She's my daughter. She's only three. She'll be scared to death if I'm not there."

"She's in the preschool at the church, right? They'll take care of the kids."

"No. I'm going after her."

"Use your head. You can't help Layla if you get yourself killed." He grasped her wrist, holding tight.

Maya struggled, twisting her arm till it hurt. "Let me go. I'm going to my baby. She's all I've got."

"That's crazy! If the hail doesn't knock you out cold the tornado's likely to bury you."

"I don't care."

"Yes, you do."

"No, I don't! Let go of me." To her amazement, he held fast. This was the kind of crude treatment she'd refused to accept in the past and had thought she'd escaped for good. No one, especially a man, was going to treat her this way and get away with it. No one.

"Stop. Think," he shouted, staring at her as if she were deranged.

She continued to struggle, to refuse to give in to his will, his greater strength. "No. *You* think. I'm going to my little girl. That's all there is to it."

"How? Driving?" He indicated the street, which now looked distorted from the vibrations of the front window. "It's too late. Look at those cars. Your head isn't half as hard as that metal is and it's already full of dents."

"But…"

She knew in her mind that he was right, yet her heart kept insisting she must do something. Anything. *Please, God, help me. Tell me what to do!*

"We're going to take shelter," Gregory ordered, giving her arm a tug. "Now."

She couldn't think and stumbled along as he pulled and half dragged her toward the basement access.

Staring into the storm moments ago she had felt as if the fury of the weather was sucking her into a bottomless black hole. Her emotions were still trapped in those murky, imaginary depths, still sinking, spinning out of control. She pictured Layla, with her silky, long dark hair and beautiful brown eyes.

"If anything happens to my daughter I'll never forgive you!" she screamed at him.

"I'll take my chances."

Maya knew without a doubt that if her precious little girl was hurt she'd never forgive herself for not trying to reach her. To protect her. And she'd never forgive Gregory Garrison for stopping her. *Never.*

She had to blink to adjust to the dim light of the basement as he shoved her in front of him and forced her down the wooden stairs.

She gasped, coughed. The place smelled musty and sour, totally in character with the advanced age of the building. How long could that strip of brick-and-stone stores and offices stand against a storm like this? If these walls ever started to topple, nothing would stop their total collapse. Then, it wouldn't matter whether they were outside or down here. They'd be just as dead.

That realization sapped her strength, leaving her almost without sensation. When her boss let go of her wrist and slipped his arm around her shoulders to guide her into a corner, she was too emotionally numb to continue to fight him. All she could do was pray and continue to repeat "Layla, Layla" over and over again.

"We'll wait it out here," he said. "This has to be the strongest part of the building."

Maya didn't believe a word he said.

Tommy's quiet sobbing, coupled with her soul-deep concern for her little girl, brought tears to her eyes. She blinked them back, hoping she could control her emotions enough to fool the boy into believing they were all going to come through the tornado unhurt.

As for herself, she wasn't sure. Not even the tiniest bit. All she could think about was her daughter. *Dear Lord, are You watching out for Layla? Please, please, please! Take care of my precious little girl.*

Chapter Two

Upstairs, the noise of the storm was increasing drastically. Things crashed. Banged. Glass shattered. Dust was shaken from the rafters. Bits of old plaster and goodness knows what else rained down on them. The single overhead bulb swung wildly, flickered, then went out, leaving the basement in total darkness.

Instinctively, Greg pulled Maya closer. She put her arms around both him and Tommy and bowed her head against his shoulder.

He felt her tremble. "Hang on. We'll be okay."

"But what'll happen to my baby? You

shouldn't have stopped me. I shouldn't have let you."

He accepted the rancor in her tone because he knew his decision to take shelter had been the right one. "You'll feel differently once we look upstairs. I wouldn't be surprised if this is the worst tornado outbreak High Plains has seen since the big one in 1860."

He felt her shudder. "That would be *devastating*."

"Exactly."

Tommy was still sniffling. Greg didn't have much experience with kids but he supposed the little boy was as concerned about his missing dog as Maya was about her family and friends. He knew he would have been at that age.

He was about to try to encourage Maya by mentioning the short-lived character of such storms when the building suddenly began to shake. Heavy wooden beams creaked and groaned overhead. Furniture, or something just as weighty, was being thrown and skidded across the office and hit the walls directly above their heads!

Maya screamed and pressed her cheek to his chest, holding tight.

The noise increased until it sounded as if a jet plane was taking off and flying right over their heads. The pressure in his eardrums made him feel as if he were rapidly descending a mountain road.

"Tornado!" Greg shouted.

Her shrill "I know!" was muted against his shoulder.

Time slowed to a crawl. Sounds of destruction seemed to echo endlessly.

Maya's heartfelt pleas for deliverance were barely audible, but Greg could tell she was praying. He was tempted to do the same until his memories stopped him. He had decided long ago that he was in charge of his own destiny and nothing had happened since to change his mind. Let the woman pray if she thought it helped. He knew better.

Maya's thoughts focused first and foremost on her daughter, then on the rest of her family. Jesse was running the Logan ranch north and west of town. He and Clay were all the blood relations she had besides Layla—and Jesse's newborn triplets, of course.

If anything good was to come out of this terrible storm, perhaps it would provide enough incentive to draw Clay home again, to cause him to make his peace with Jesse. It tore her up to see her only siblings estranged from each other, especially now that Jesse and his wife, Marie, had three premature babies to worry about, too.

She tried to pray aloud, failed to find words, then resorted to quoting scripture. "The cares of the day are sufficient," she whispered, hoping that would help relieve her unbelievable distress.

She felt Greg's muscles tense. He stood very still, barely breathing. "What?"

"It's from the Bible. In Matthew, I think. My paraphrasing." She cringed against him again and stifled a whimper as the building gave another shimmy. The roaring was starting to lessen enough that they could hear each other speak without having to actually shout.

"I wouldn't know if it was verbatim," he

said. "I never went to church much after my mother died."

"That's too bad."

"It didn't do *her* much good."

Touched, Maya gave him a barely perceptible hug. "We won't know that until we get to Heaven."

Although he didn't answer, she was glad she'd spoken her mind. Gregory Garrison might not claim to be a believer at present, but since he'd gone to church in the past, there was a chance he'd eventually come around again. She certainly hoped so because she couldn't imagine the suffering he might have to go through if he continued to deny his faith. Especially if the destruction from this storm turned out to be as bad as she thought it was going to be.

Everyone had doubts at times, even the most devout Christians. It was those who continued to believe, in spite of outward circumstances, who coped best.

And as far as she was concerned, any man who would risk his own life to save a child he didn't even *like* still deserved to share in the Lord's daily blessings.

* * *

Greg held tight to the two he was guarding and listened to the battering on the floor and walls above. He desperately wanted to venture out, yet he wasn't willing to endanger Maya or the boy merely to satisfy his curiosity.

Tommy had stopped sobbing and was now hugging Greg's neck as if he never intended to let go, while Maya seemed to be holding her breath.

Finally, as the thudding and banging upstairs lessened perceptibly, his impatience won out. "I'm going to go take a peek. You two wait here. I'll tell you if it's safe to follow me upstairs."

When he pried the child's arms loose and passed him to Maya, Tommy began to sob again.

"We'll go up in a few minutes," Maya said soothingly, patting the little boy's back through his damp T-shirt. "I promise. We have to let Mr. Garrison look around first to see if it's safe."

"I w-want Charlie," Tommy wailed. "I want my dog."

"I know you do, honey. Just be a little patient. I'll help you look for Charlie soon." She looked in her boss's direction. "We both will, won't we?"

"Yeah. Sure." He had started to cautiously edge his way toward the stairway. "Sounds like the wind is still pretty strong. No telling how much is blowing around up there but I suspect the worst is over."

"I hope so."

He put one hand on the railing of the stairway and paused. "So far, so good. You'll have a little light once I open the door. Are you going to be all right down here by yourself?"

"I won't be alone," she replied, sounding more assured than before. "I haven't had to face anything on my own since I came to Jesus."

Greg didn't comment. He'd grown up in a household where his mother had professed Christianity and his father had made light of it every chance he got. There weren't many things he agreed with his dad about, but that was one of them. Any God who would take his mother from them in the prime of her life, in spite of all the prayers for her healing, was no God for him.

Easing open the door at the top of the stairs, he had to push its leading edge through a pile of refuse on the floor. The office was a shambles, thanks to the wind that was still whistling through the gap left by the shattered plate-glass window. The front door was hanging partly off its hinges, too. Considering the fact that his building was still standing, he figured he was one of the lucky ones. Especially if the upstairs suite where he currently lived still had a roof over it.

Stepping through and around the rubble, he proceeded far enough to peer through the space where the window glass had been. All his breath left him in a whoosh. He'd never seen anything like it. Parked cars had been upended like matchbox toys. Lumber, pink insulation, broken furniture and who knows what lay strewn from one end of Main Street to the other. Some of it was even stuck in trees. What was left of them.

Behind him, he heard Maya call, "Is it okay for us to come up?"

"Not yet." There was no way he could deny her the eventual right to look, nor was there any way he could soften the blow of seeing their beloved town in such sad shape. He simply wanted to put it off as long as possible and keep her from dashing into the still unsafe street.

"Give me a few seconds to run upstairs and check my apartment first. We need to be sure there's no real structural damage before you chance it. I don't want the roof caving in on us."

"Hurry." He could hear the barely controlled panic in her voice.

"I will. Stay put till I call you. Promise?"

"I promise."

Greg dashed up the interior stairway. To his relief the roof seemed intact and he'd had only one small window cracked in his apartment, so the place was relatively dry and undamaged.

Hoping that Maya had obeyed, he quickly returned and found her peeking through the partially ajar cellar door.

"Well?" she asked impatiently.

"It's safe enough. At least in here. But

watch your step and don't put the boy down unless you have to. There's broken glass everywhere."

He braced himself, not sure how Maya would react when she saw everything that had happened. If she got hysterical, the way she had earlier, he'd have to be ready to intervene.

For the first time in the few weeks she'd worked for him, Greg looked—really looked—at his executive assistant. Her dark eyes were wide and expressive, set in a lovely oval face. Her short hair was tousled more than usual. And her cheeks were flushed. She not only impressed him with her natural beauty, she suddenly looked much younger than the twenty-five years he knew her to be. She had an innocence, an appealing naïveté, that made her seem so vulnerable that he wanted to rush to her and once again hold her close for her protection.

Maya's jaw gaped. Then she began to pick her way carefully across the wet, littered office floor to join him near the window.

"The church?" she said breathlessly.

"Can you see if the community church is still standing?"

"Yes. It looks fine," Greg replied. "But the old town hall that was next to it is gone."

"*Gone?* It can't be gone."

"I'm sorry." He stepped aside and took Tommy from her so she could lean far enough to see the area where the old church stood as he said, "The preschool annex looks untouched, too."

"Praise God! I have to get Layla."

"You can't go out there yet." He made ready to grab and restrain her again if it became necessary. "Look. There are power lines down and the wind is still blowing stuff all over. If you don't get electrocuted, you're liable to get your head knocked off."

"It's my head. Get out of my way. I'm going."

"No!" He reached for her arm but she dodged his grip so he resorted to more reasoning. "You're the only parent your daughter has. Are you really willing to risk making her an orphan?"

"Of course not."

"Then wait. Think of her."

"I am thinking of her. She needs me. You can't force me to stay here."

"I'm not forcing you to do anything. Be sensible. We can see that the church is okay and that's where she was. Right?" Greg had placed himself between her and the door in the hopes his presence would be enough added deterrent.

Maya ignored his logical argument and tried to edge around him.

He sidestepped to continue to block her exit.

"Move," she demanded.

"Okay. Just take a deep breath and listen to me for a second. We're safe here and Layla is safe there. She needs her mother alive and well, not lying in the street unconscious."

"I'm calling the preschool."

"Now, you're being smart."

He watched her struggle to pull herself together emotionally and tiptoe cautiously to where her desk had landed, pushed up against the far wall. She found the telephone beside it on the floor and lifted the receiver. It didn't surprise him when she reported, "No dial tone."

"Try my cell if you can find it," Greg said. "It was in my top, center drawer."

Maya circled his heavier mahogany desk, yanked open the drawer with difficulty, found the cell phone and did as he'd suggested.

Dejected, she grimaced, sighed and shook her head. "No service on that, either."

"I suppose the relay towers are down."

"That settles it. I'm going over to the church and nobody's going to stop me."

"Then we'll all go," he countered.

"That's ridiculous. You can't take Tommy out in this awful wind. He'll get hurt."

"Point taken. Now, you were saying…?"

"All right, all right." Maya pressed her lips into a thin line. "You win. For now. But the minute the storm dies down enough that we can safely chance it, I'm going after my little girl. With or without your support."

Even if Greg had been able to come up with a more valid argument, he wouldn't have used it. Maya was like a mother tiger protecting her cub, and he was not about to get between her and her daughter.

Still, he knew without a doubt that his instincts were on target. She must be prevented from risking her well-being. He didn't know why he felt so protective of her all of a sudden but he did. And he was stubborn enough to insist on getting his way. This time.

In the next war of wills they faced, maybe he'd let her win, or at least think she had. In this case, however, he was not about to back down. Lives hung in the balance.

As Maya stood beside her boss and stared at the havoc the storm had wrought, she was speechless. Breathless.

The town gazebo had become a scattered mass of wood that looked like a carelessly tossed handful of splintered matchsticks.

The usually pristine, well-manicured green grass of the park that paralleled Main Street and bordered the High Plains River on the opposite side was strewn with all kinds of materials, including puffy, pink shreds of fiberglass insulation that had apparently been torn from houses nearby. To release that kind of interior construction, Maya knew that roofs and sidewalls of homes had to have been ripped apart.

And the formerly beautiful trees. She was astounded. "What a shame. Look at the poor cottonwoods."

"All the more proof that you wouldn't have made it to the church in one piece," he reminded her.

She hated to agree but he was right. Many of the trees that had lined the riverbank had been toppled, with nearly their entire root balls sticking out of the ground. Those that were still standing had limbs broken away or their whole tops twisted off. The remaining leafless branches were draped with black tar paper and other flexible materials that flapped frantically like ugly, misshapen flags.

Sheets of corrugated tin had been ripped from roofs and bent tightly around the windward side of the more substantial portions of some of the trees, as if squeezed in place by a giant, malevolent hand. If no one in or around High Plains had been killed in this storm it would be a wonder.

Raising her gaze to the horizon across the river, she gasped. Her hand flew to her throat. The danger wasn't over. Her boss had been right about that, too. A wall cloud lay just above the northern hills. And it looked as if it was located directly over her brother Jesse's Circle L Ranch!

As she watched, the solid line at the bottom of the black horizontal wall fractured. Dark masses began to drop lower into the lighter sky in several places. At first they just looked like more clouds.

Then, one of them became a finger of spinning chaos and snaked downward, moving as if it were a double-jointed talon with a razor-sharp claw at its base, ready to tear at the land below. To rip everything it touched to shreds. To kill anything—anyone—in its path.

Dear Jesus. Maya prayed, pointing, trembling. "Another tornado!"

"I see it." He slipped his free arm around her shoulders and gave her a supportive squeeze. "Don't worry. That one's a long way from here. Judging by the direction everything is moving, it won't come anywhere near us."

"I know," Maya replied, having to fight the lump in her throat in order to speak. "But my oldest brother and his family live out there."

"Where?"

She shivered, glad he had hold of her as she took a shaky breath and made herself say, "Right at the base of that funnel cloud."

Greg wished he could control nature, make the storm go away for good. Fortunately, the overall turbulence didn't seem as if it was going to last much longer.

As they stood and watched, the snaking cord of the latest funnel cloud thinned, broke into sections, then retreated back into the ominous ebony cloud cover until there was no more sign of it.

The worst of the local wind and rain had tapered off, too, leaving stifling humidity. Greg wasn't sure whether he was still soggy from his trip outside to rescue Tommy or if he was beginning to perspire, now that there was no electricity to run the air-conditioning. Probably both.

He looked Maya up and down, ending his perusal at her feet. "You'll need some sensible shoes if we're going to hike to the church from here. Are those all you have?"

"They'll be fine. I'm used to wearing heels."

"I know you are. The problem is the mess in the street, not your shoes."

"I used to keep an old pair of sneakers in the trunk of my car. Unfortunately, I took them out last week."

"I doubt it matters. Have you checked our parking lot?" He had not done so, either, yet judging by the damage to Main Street, the area at the rear of nearby stores and offices was probably just as big a disaster. If her car happened to be drivable, which was doubtful, there would still be no safe routes in or around High Plains, at least not for a while.

"You know I haven't." She made a face at him. "Is there anything else you'd like to ask? Because if you're done criticizing me, I want to get started."

"I wasn't criticizing you, I was being rational. We obviously can't drive through all this debris, so we'll have to walk. And the easiest way to get hurt is to not be sure-footed enough. You may have to climb or jump." He studied her tailored outfit, making note of her slim skirt. "Do you think you can do that?"

"I can do *anything* that will get me to my daughter," Maya said emphatically. "I'm going now, whether you come or not."

Tommy wiggled in Greg's arms so he lowered him to the floor, keeping hold of his thin wrist so he wouldn't run away.

"Let go," the child whined. "I have to go find Charlie. He might be hurt."

Lots of people might be, Greg thought. He said, "We'll all look for your dog while we walk over to the church to get Ms. Logan's little girl. Maybe Charlie went there to guard all the other kids." He could tell by Maya's grim expression that she wasn't buying his theory but as long as Tommy did, that was good enough for Greg.

"O-okay. But if we see Charlie he gets to come, too."

"Absolutely," Maya told him, taking his hand and bending to look him in the eyes. "You have to be really good for Mr. Garrison and me, okay? It's very dangerous out there and if you got hurt, you couldn't keep looking for Charlie. Do you understand?"

The child nodded soberly, amazing Greg with his sudden acceptance of adult authority. Apparently, if there was a valid reason to obey, Tommy was capable of controlling himself enough to do so. He just wished Maya had interceded in that sane and practical manner before the wild kid had splashed mud all over the sidewalk.

Realizing how trivial his thoughts were in light of the disaster that had just descended upon High Plains, Greg began to chuckle quietly.

Maya arched her eyebrows and gave him a withering look. "What in the world is so funny?"

"I am," he said, shaking his head and following with more self-deprecating laughter. "I was just thinking about not wanting mud splashed on my office. Right now, I'd willingly settle for a little mud on the outside if that was all that was wrong."

"I know what you mean," she said. "But if you keep me standing here wasting time for one more minute I'm going to scream. Are you ready to go?"

"As ready as I'll ever be."

He left Tommy in her care as he shouldered the damaged front door to force it partway open. Then he motioned and held out his hand.

When she took it to let him assist her and the boy through the narrow opening, he noticed that her slim fingers were clammy and trembling. Considering how scared she must be, especially in regard to her daughter, she was handling her feelings pretty well.

Greg hadn't been a praying man for a long, long time, but under the circumstances he was tempted to try it, just this once. All he wanted to ask was that Maya's bravery be honored by a safe reunion with her child. If her God really existed, really cared, she deserved that much at the very least.

Chapter Three

Maya would have run all the way to the church if there had been any way to safely do so. Stepping gingerly and wending her way through the rubble, she was awestruck. So many loose building bricks littered what had once been the sidewalk they had to take to the center of the street in order to pass.

Whole structures had collapsed, and many of those that hadn't actually fallen had been stripped of portions of their facade, making them barely recognizable.

Broken glass lay everywhere. Cars were smashed, some lying on the sidewalks and lawns where they'd been dropped like discarded toys. Since she couldn't see any occupants inside the wrecks she could only hope their drivers had sensibly run for cover before the worst of the storm had overtaken them.

Piles of jagged refuse were heaped against the windward sides of anything solid, not to mention the rubbish floating in the High Plains River, near where the lovely, quaint gazebo had stood mere minutes ago.

Greg put out his hand and stopped her. "Wait here with Tommy a second. I think I see movement inside the pie shop. They might be trapped."

There was no way Maya could bring herself to argue with him when he was bent on doing a good deed. All she said was, "Hurry."

She knew without a doubt that people could be hurt all over town. Dying. Suffering. That thought cut her to the quick. Many of her friends and neighbors might be in dire straits—perhaps even worse—not to mention her brother Jesse. For the first time since the onset of the tornado, Maya thought of the Garrison family, too.

As soon as he returned and reported that

the folks in Elmira's diner were all right she asked, "Do you think your father is okay?"

"Probably. He's too mean to die."

"What an awful thing to say!"

"Just quoting him," Greg answered, continuing to lead the way east along Main Street. "He's been saying that for years. Besides, the estate is pretty far out of town. I don't imagine it was in the storm's path. At least not this time."

"I wish I could say the same for the Logan ranch," she replied. "I suppose there won't be any way to tell how Jesse and Marie are until communication is restored."

"Maybe we can hitch a quick ride out that way later and you can see for yourself."

She shook her head, then pointed. "Not unless that bridge is in better shape than it looks from here. The whole roadway is blocked up by big pieces of houses and goodness knows what else."

"You're right. That probably means the rescue units from the other side of the river won't be able to get to us without going miles out of their way, either."

"I know." She sighed. "It's going to take

us weeks just to dig out, and that will be only the beginning. No wonder so many people are just wandering around in a daze. It boggles my mind, too."

"I can help with the rebuilding," Greg told her, leading their little group in a circuitous path that avoided loose wires that were dangling between battered telephone poles. "My lumber yard and hardware wholesale can supply resources, even if they've sustained some damage."

"That should be profitable, too."

Maya knew she shouldn't have taken his offer so negatively but she'd worked for the man long enough to know that he was fixated on the bottom line: net gains. It wasn't his fault that that was the way his mind worked, but she did see it as the reason he'd been so successful when he was barely thirty.

He sobered and glowered at her. "This isn't about business, it's about survival. I'm not going to try to make money from the misfortunes of others, even if my father's opinion of me suffers as a result."

"He wouldn't understand?"

"No. That old man has never approved of

anything I've done, which is the main reason I told him I was leaving High Plains for keeps, years ago."

"It must have been hard for you to come back."

"Yes, it was. If my cousin Michael hadn't phoned and told me Dad was terminally ill, I'd still be enjoying my studio apartment with a view of Lake Michigan, instead of standing in the middle of this horrible mess."

"With me," Maya added, giving his strong hand a squeeze. "I'm really sorry you have to go through all this but I'm glad you're here. If you hadn't been, who knows what would have become of me in this storm."

"I hope you'd have had the good sense to duck."

Maya nodded. "Yeah. Me, too. But I doubt it."

Reverend Michael Garrison, Greg's cousin, was also pastor of the largest house of worship in town, the three-story High Plains Community Church.

By the time Greg, Maya and Tommy arrived on the church grounds, Michael had his shirtsleeves rolled up and was standing outside the historic, white-sided wooden building, offering solace and sanctuary to passersby.

Tall, slim and darker-haired than Greg, he greeted everyone with open arms, then shook Greg's hand as Maya left with Tommy and hurried toward the annex where the pre-school was located.

"How does it look over here?" Greg asked Michael. "Are the church and preschool okay?"

"Fine, fine," the pastor answered. "Maya's daughter is a wonder. She came through the storm like a trooper. All the kids did. The last time I looked, Layla was helping Josie and Nicki comfort the most frightened little ones."

"Sounds tough and capable, just like her mama," Greg said proudly. He scanned the church. "I can't believe those big stained-glass windows survived."

"They have safety glass over them, thanks to our insurance company's insistence."

"How about the parsonage out back? Do you still have a place to live?"

"Yes. It's fine, too."

"Good. Well, if you don't need me right now I'll go see how Maya's faring. Is there anything else I can help you with first?"

"Not that I can think of," Michael replied, looking weary and old far beyond his twenty-eight years. "I'm still trying to get my head around all this. We lost the carriage house, right down to the foundation, so we can't use it for temporary housing the way we used to."

"What are you going to do?"

"Move survivors into the fellowship hall in the church basement for the time being. I've already got half a dozen women working in the kitchen, preparing food as best they can without electricity."

Greg brightened. "There are a few generators in stock at my hardware store. If we can get to them and they still work after all this, they're yours."

"God bless you." Michael clapped him on the back with affection. "I knew we could count on your help. I'm glad you were here."

"Yeah. I've been told that same thing once already. I'm not sure I should be happy about it but it does seem advantageous."

"The good Lord works in mysterious ways."

"Well, maybe. Just don't start trying to tell me I'm back in High Plains because it's God's will, okay?"

Grinning and looking a lot better than he had when Greg had first walked up, Michael said, "Perish the thought."

Greg was still digesting his cousin's last comment when he reached the door to the preschool. Its handmade sign was hanging by one edge and flapping in the breeze, but other than that and some deep dings in the paint on the lapped wood siding, it looked unscathed.

He shuddered. Given the fact that he could better assess what little was left of the carriage house and old town hall from where he stood, it was phenomenal that the historic church—and the children inside the annex—had been spared. This tornado had come way too close for comfort.

Greg was reaching for the knob when the door flew open and Tommy ran out, barreling into him.

"Whoa. Where do you think you're going?" Greg caught the small, wiry child and swung him into his arms.

"Let me go. I gotta find Charlie."

"We'll go, we'll go. I just need to tell Maya, I mean Ms. Logan, and her daughter what's going on."

He stepped into the doorway to scan the room. In view of the mess the children had made while playing on the floor, it was hard to tell that the tornado had actually skipped over their facility. Greg smiled when his gaze found Maya's.

"She's fine. Layla's fine," Maya called out, waving excitedly. "Come on in."

Greg shook his head. "Can't right now. Tommy and I are going to go looking for Charlie, like we promised, and I need to stop by the hardware store, too. Michael needs a generator."

"Then we'll come with you," Maya said quickly and firmly. "I want to see what's left of my house and check on some friends. We can drop Tommy by his foster parents' house on the way. The Otises live over on First Street, across from the schools."

"Are you sure you're up to it?" Greg eyed her feet once again.

"Yes, I'm sure. I got here in one piece and

I can get back the way we came just as well as you can. Besides, if I want any other shoes, I have to go home to get them."

"That sounds reasonable." He had to tighten his grip on the wiggly boy. "Hurry it up. Tommy's giving me fits."

"When has he *not?*" With Layla in tow she joined them at the open door. "I know I shouldn't be smiling, in view of all that's happened, but I can't help myself. I'm just so happy to be with my daughter again."

"I imagine a lot of folks feel that way. I hardly know what to think or do myself. This whole picture is too unbelievable to take in all at once. Half of me wants to mourn while the other half can't help grinning about the most inane things."

"The buildings can be rebuilt," she said wisely. "It's the people I care about who worry me now. And I'm sure Tommy's foster parents are beside themselves."

"Maybe Charlie went home," the boy piped up. "He has a dog house and everything."

"That sounds wonderful," Maya said.

She lifted her small daughter and they

started to leave the church grounds together. Yes, the dog may have survived, he told himself. In view of the loss of the gazebo and many of the other structures in the vicinity where they'd last spotted the scraggly mutt, however, it was iffy. Then again, if Charlie was half as streetwise as Greg thought he was, he could also be in the next county— or farther—by now.

Unfortunately, he may have been so frightened by the turbulence and devastation he might never decide to come back.

Maya's arms and back ached from toting the three-year-old on first one hip, then the other, yet she refused to put her down.

"I can walk," Layla kept insisting.

"I know you can, honey. But it's too dangerous, especially since you're wearing shorts and sandals. Look at all the nails and sharp, pointy things that can hurt you. Mama needs to carry you just a bit farther."

"Um, I'm not real used to kids but I suppose I can take her for you if you need a break," Greg offered.

"No. I'm fine. I don't mind a bit."

"You just don't want to let go of her, right?"

Maya had to smile. "How did you know?"

"It's basic human nature. You're her mother and you need to be close to her right now."

"Boy, is that the truth." She sobered. "Look at all this. I don't even know where to think of beginning."

"The rescuers are starting their searches," her boss observed. "I saw one of the patrol cars wrecked back there but apparently there are enough undamaged police units and fire trucks to get the job done. At least I hope so."

"Surely, there will be others coming in, too."

"That's true."

"How will we get that generator back to Reverend Michael?"

"Don't worry. I'll arrange something." He was eyeing the upper story of the Garrison Building as they passed it and turned down First Street. "Thankfully, I won't have much cleaning up to do."

Maya gasped. "Oh, I'm so sorry. I should have asked. Is your apartment damaged? If it is, I'll help you with it. I promise."

"It's fine. Let's worry about one thing at

a time." He glanced across the street. "Access to the front of the hardware store and the parking lot looks blocked but I can probably find a few good old boys with trucks and winches to get past the clutter."

He waved to a small group of his employees who were gathered in the street. "Is everybody okay?"

"Fine, Mr. Garrison. We were getting ready to close. No customers at all."

"That's good. Try to get to our spare generators, will you? I want the biggest one delivered to Reverend Michael at High Plains Community Church, ASAP. No charge. And grab a half dozen extension cords to go with it. Okay?"

"Okay. I'll try to get a little gas for it, too. Anything else?"

"Yes. See if you can find a volunteer to man what's left of the store so folks can get whatever they need—at cost—whether they have the money for it or not. Just write everything down and we'll work out the details later."

"Gotcha. I can stay. I live so far west of town I'm sure the storm missed my place."

"Good." Looking satisfied, Gregory

turned back to Maya. "How much farther is it to Tommy's?"

"Just down there. I can see the house. Praise the Lord! It's still standing." She could tell that her boss was having to work to keep hold of the struggling boy's arm.

"Whoa, kid. Hold your horses. I'll let you go in just a second."

"Charlie!" Tommy kept yelling. "Charlie. Charlie, where are you?"

Maya looked up and down the street, hoping against hope that the black-and-white mutt would suddenly appear. Very little was moving other than the refuse that flapped in the trees and lay draped over every bush and signpost, as if naughty teenagers had arrayed it like toilet paper in a prank. Sadly, this was no childish practical joke. This was harsh reality.

Green-painted shutters had been ripped from the quaint Otis home and there were spaces on the sloping roof that were clearly missing patches of asphalt shingles. Other than that, the house looked in pretty good shape, especially compared to some of the others they'd seen so far.

Gregory released the boy and Tommy

raced ahead, vaulting a low hedge that bordered the backyard of his foster parents.

Holding Layla close, Maya paused to watch. A dog house lay on its side with a chain tether still attached. The rest of the yard was deserted. Charlie was nowhere to be seen.

Tears came to her eyes as she heard the child start to sob. His loud weeping immediately drew Beth and Brandon from the house and they fell to their knees to embrace him.

At least Tommy was safe, Maya thought, thanks to the quick actions of Gregory Garrison. And this was probably only one of the many happy reunions occurring all over the area.

She'd never thought to pray for an animal before but considering the heartbreaking agony the poor, lonely little boy was in, she couldn't see a thing wrong with doing so now.

"Father, thank You for saving us," she began to whisper. "And please help Tommy find his dog."

At her ear, hugging her neck tightly, she heard her three-year-old add, "Amen."

Middle-aged, slight portly, Brandon Otis was the first to approach and offer his hand to Greg. "Thanks for bringing him home. We were pretty upset."

"I can see that," Greg said, noting a slight tremor in the man's grip. "No sign of the dog?"

Brandon shook his head. "Nope. None." He leaned closer and lowered his voice to add aside, "That's the least of my worries. Beth doesn't say much but I think her old ticker is acting up again. Wouldn't be surprised after what we just went through."

That took Greg aback. "Your wife is ill?"

"The only times it bothers her is when she's stressed, like now. And having Tommy's dog here hasn't helped. We just didn't have the heart to refuse to let him bring it."

"How is that a problem?"

The older man huffed in disgust. "We had a fight just about every night over bringing Charlie inside. We always said no, but half the time he ended up sleeping in Tommy's bed with him anyway. Poor Beth had more laundry from this kid than a dozen of the ones we'd fostered before him."

"I had just assumed Charlie was your dog."

"No way. Beth's allergic. The only reason we gave in was because the authorities swore Tommy would be lost without it." He gestured. "I even built a dog house with a tie-out chain. See? Not that Charlie spent much time there."

"Tommy was riding a bike downtown when the storm hit. Charlie was with him then. Afterward, we couldn't find him and we'd hoped he'd wandered back this way."

"Nope. Sorry. Haven't seen hide nor hair of him."

Disappointed, Greg left Brandon and stepped over the low hedge into the Otises' backyard. As he approached, Beth stood, wiped her eyes and went to join her husband, Maya and Layla.

The boy was sitting on the grass with his face in his hands, oblivious to the wet ground, when Greg crouched next to him.

"I'm sorry," was all Greg said. That was apparently enough.

Tommy looked up. His eyes were red and his face puffy and tear-stained. He paused a moment to stare, then got up and threw his arms around Greg, catching him by surprise and nearly bowling him over.

"Nobody cares," the boy wailed.

Astounded by the intense reaction, Greg nevertheless recovered enough to embrace the child and try to comfort him. He was in way over his head. He didn't know how to handle kids, what to say to them or how to help. He just knew that Tommy's suffering was touching his heart with a depth of feeling he hadn't known existed.

As soon as the child's sobbing lessened enough that he could heed spoken assurances, Greg said, "I care. And so does Ms. Logan."

"Charlie's my—my only friend," Tommy stuttered, sniffling. "He's my best buddy. We go everywhere together."

"Then I know he'll come back if he can," Greg said sympathetically.

The boy's blue eyes widened. "What if

he's hurt like my mama and daddy were? They *never* came back."

"There are going to be lots of people out looking for ways to help each other in the next few days and weeks, son. I'm sure someone will find your dog. And we'll look especially hard for him, just like we promised."

"You—you will? Cross your heart?"

Greg made the motion that went with the question as he replied, "Yes. Cross my heart."

In truth, he felt as if his heart was breaking for this sad, lonely child. Remembering his own youth he could readily identify with Tommy. There had been no one in his young life at the Garrison estate who had understood him except his mother, and when she'd died he'd been so bereft that no words could describe it. Although he'd still had a father, Dan had become even more withdrawn than usual, leaving Greg feeling totally isolated.

In those days, if he hadn't had some animals to tend, to talk to without censoring his thoughts and words, he'd have been as forlorn as Tommy was now.

Blinking, he fought back the tears that had

so unexpectedly filled his eyes. He didn't know how they were going to find the missing dog, or if they ever would. Only one thing was certain. He was going to try as hard as possible.

Maya kept peeking past Beth's shoulder at the astonishing scene taking place in the Otises' yard. If someone had asked her an hour ago whether she thought Gregory Garrison even liked children, let alone empathized with them, she would have flatly denied that possibility.

Now, however, she was witnessing a show of compassion from her crusty boss that she could barely believe. Not only was he comforting Tommy, he was doing so on his knees in a wet, muddy yard despite his expensive slacks.

Then again, she mused, the rest of his suit was already ruined back at the office, so she guessed it didn't matter much. It was amazing what things no longer did, such as keeping her hair looking neat or her shoes polished, not to mention making sure her own yard was tidy.

Maya shuddered as she contemplated

going home. *Assuming I still have a home,* she added silently.

Her conscience reared up and kicked her. *Things* could be replaced. People could not. She should be praising the Lord and thanking Him that they had all survived instead of worrying about lost or damaged possessions.

Smiling slightly, she took another peek at her boss and Tommy. They had separated. Greg was getting to his feet. He offered his hand to the boy and they shook solemnly, apparently sealing a gentlemen's agreement.

Maya was so touched by that tender sight she almost wept. A big, strong man was treating a frightened little boy as his equal.

Never again would she view Gregory Garrison in the same light as before. He might deny it—and probably would—but he really was a nice, nice man under all that sternness and supposed perfectionism.

And he had just earned himself a place among those few special, extraordinary individuals whom she most admired.

Of all the shocks this day had brought, that was certainly one of the most meaningful.

Chapter Four

Maya waited patiently with Layla until Beth and her husband had ushered Tommy into the house and Greg had come back across the hedge.

"Well, what's next?" he asked. "How far is it to your place?"

"About a block and a half. I live at Logan and Second Streets, past the elementary school grounds."

"Do you want to walk on over and see how your house fared?"

She shrugged and grimaced. "I'm not sure. I want to see, but I don't, if you know what I mean."

"I certainly do." He gestured down the

narrow sidewalk, then held out his arms to Layla. "May I have the honor of carrying you, Princess?"

The three-year-old giggled. Maya could tell that her daughter wouldn't mind if Greg took her for a while so she passed her to him with a smile. "I thought you didn't like children."

"I admit I haven't had much experience with them but I wouldn't go so far as to say I don't like them. Let's just say they're a mystery to me."

"Fair enough. Thanks for offering. She was getting heavy."

"And you're stressed out, besides," he said. "You didn't bring your purse. Do you have a house key with you?"

"Don't need one. I never lock my doors. Besides, my purse is safer in my desk drawer than it would be if I were hauling it all over town with me."

"That makes sense. You'll feel better once you've seen your place and gotten some sensible clothes and shoes."

Maya knew he was just chatting to try to distract her from the harsh reality of the

tornado's destruction, but his constant re-
minders were getting old fast. "I know, I
know. As you've said before, I need to
change before I can be of any use cleaning
up." Meeting his gaze and sensing his
thoughts she was instantly penitent. "Sorry.
I didn't mean to snap at you. It's been a
rough day."

"For everybody," he countered. "And I do
understand. Thank goodness we have insurance." He hesitated, studying her expression.
"You did have your house insured, didn't
you?"

"Well, sort of. I had been meaning to
increase the coverage. You know how it is.
That place has stood there for more than
seventy-five years, through all kinds of
weather. I never thought anything would
happen to it."

"We don't know that it has," he replied.

"No, not yet. But I've had a bad feeling
about it ever since we were hiding in the
basement." She pointed. "Look at the elementary school. See that pile of tar paper?
Half its roof must be lying in the street."

Filled with more foreboding by the

second, she skirted a downed limb that bridged the sidewalk, then hurried ahead to the corner.

All her breath left her in a whoosh of relief. *Praise the Lord!* Judging by what she could see from there, her house was in pretty good shape. The gabled roofline was intact and the windows on that side seemed solid.

She turned back to her boss with a smile. "Wow. It looks okay. I can't believe it."

Together, they proceeded down Logan Street. Several other homes were slightly damaged to the same degree the Otis house had been. Other than that, and the partially denuded trees along the frontage areas, there was actually little destruction showing.

As they neared Maya's home, however, she began to glimpse loose boards and insulation littering her side yard. Beginning to jog ahead, she soon knew the full, awful truth that had been hidden behind the untouched portions of the old house.

By the time the others caught up to her she was standing on the soggy carpeting where her living room had been and looking at the gray sky that was visible through the remaining ceiling beams and roof joists.

All her boss could say was, "I'm so sorry."

She bent to retrieve a small pink teddy bear from the rubble, then dropped it when it streamed rainwater. "I knew it. I just knew it."

"What about the rest of the place?" he asked. "Do you want to watch Layla while I check it for you?"

"What?" Maya had heard him speak but her mind was so focused on the incredible damage she'd barely taken in his question, let alone processed it.

"I said, do you want me to check the rest of the house?"

"I don't know, I…" Suddenly she began to giggle.

Approaching, he gently touched her forearm. "What is it? Are you okay?"

Maya nodded while she continued laughing. Soon, tears were streaming down her cheeks.

"I'm fine," she finally managed to say. Waving her hands in front of her, palms out, she struggled to explain. "My first thought was that I didn't want you to go into the back rooms because…because I hadn't finished folding and putting away the laundry."

She was grinning inanely, she knew, but the situation was just so ridiculous—and she was so keyed up after the storm—she couldn't help herself. "I didn't want you to see the clutter. Can you believe it? I'm standing in a nonexistent living room and I'm worried about a messy bedroom. I should be thankful I even *have* a bedroom."

"I see your point," he said. "I was afraid you'd come unglued again."

"Not me," Maya replied. "I am usually one together lady in spite of my behavior earlier today. After my parents died, Clay and Jesse both said it was my sensible nature that kept our family on an even keel." She sobered. "Of course, it didn't stop my brothers from quarreling or keep Clay from leaving home. Still, I did all I could to keep the peace between them."

"I'm sure you did." He passed Layla to Maya and backed away. "If you think you can stand letting me tour your messy house—what there is of it—I'll go see if the bedrooms seem stable."

Maya nodded. "Thanks. We'll wait. I'd go myself but I don't want to expose Layla to any more dangers. I'll turn off the gas at the meter, just in case they haven't shut down service to the whole town yet."

"Good idea. Hang on and try to keep from getting too silly again. I'll be right back."

Watching him wend his way through the partially collapsed room and enter the hallway, Maya again gave thanks for Gregory Garrison's assistance.

She hadn't dreamed she'd *ever* have a casual or personal conversation with her stuffy, persnickety boss, let alone encourage him to poke through her home. Then again, there wasn't anything to hide. She had done her best to support herself and her daughter, though that had meant making many sacrifices along the way. What few possessions they did have were contained in that house. *Correction,* in what was left of it.

For an instant, she rued the loss. Then she remembered that she and Layla were alive and well and asked the Lord's forgiveness. She was grateful. Period. And no matter what happened next, she was going to make certain she never lost sight of that blessing.

Thinking of family again while she shut the gas valve, her thoughts turned to Jesse. He was almost ten years her senior, yet she had the urge to mother him, to give him a big hug and soothe his losses, assuming the second twister had actually hit the ranch, as she'd supposed.

As soon as the phones were up and working, her eldest brother was going to be the first person she called. And until then, she was going to pray for him and his family as fervently as humanly possible. The rest was up to God.

Greg found surprisingly little damage in the remaining parts of Maya's house. There were a few cracked windows and some of the ceiling plaster had fallen but other than that, the bedrooms and bath were intact.

He returned to Maya with a smile. "Looks good back there. Solid, not shaky. I think it's safe for you to go take a look."

"And change my clothes and shoes. I know," she said with a wry grin. "You don't have to tell me again."

He hoped he was managing to look suitably contrite because he wanted to make her life as easy as possible, especially right now. "Hey. I didn't say a word."

"Not this time, no."

It pleased him to see a genuine smile light her pretty face so he added, "See? I'm teachable."

"I'll reserve judgment on that. Watch Layla for me while I change, will you? I'll need to pack a few things for both of us, too, assuming they're not sopping wet. We certainly won't be able to live here."

"Probably not for a while. But I can help you rebuild if you want."

"You'd do that? For me?"

He wanted to tell her how impressed he'd been by her fortitude and unswerving courage in the face of disaster but decided it was best to keep his offer simple so he said, "Of course. We're all going to need to work together to get High Plains back on its feet. I'm sure Michael will be organizing work crews soon, and I intend to volunteer to help with whatever is necessary."

"I believe you really mean that."

Greg nodded. "I've never meant anything more."

As she left him and he held her child in his arms, he wondered how a woman alone managed to cope as well as Maya had. His mother had always seemed to defer to her husband and Dan had taken full advantage of her meekness, even when she was too sick to complain, had she wanted to. That was one of the main things for which Greg could not forgive the man.

As far as Greg was concerned, his leaving High Plains for good had been inevitable. And now? Now, here he was, back in the same small town and watching it face the worst disaster it had experienced in almost a hundred and fifty years.

He sighed. Was he up to the challenge? Of course. The real question was, why him? Why now? He didn't believe in predestination, yet there did seem to be something odd about the timing of this storm. Had it occurred a few weeks prior he probably wouldn't have come home at all.

And if it had happened after his father's impending death, the same was true. He might have come back to arrange Dan's funeral and take care of liquidating the estate but he certainly wouldn't have set up his investment business right downtown.

Truth to tell, he hadn't actually had to do that, either, given his ability to work online from just about anywhere. Nevertheless, he was glad he had opened an actual office.

The Garrison building had always been a favorite of his, due in part to its impressive architecture, and he'd easily decided to move into it. Living in a remodeled suite upstairs and working on the ground floor had seemed natural, too. The brick and limestone structure was solid and strong, prevailing against all odds, not unlike the way he viewed himself.

He glanced at the wreckage strewn across the front lawn of Maya's property and began to hope that his new secretary was a lot stronger than *her* home had been. If she wasn't, she was going to need his help even more than she had so far.

It wasn't hard for Maya to find a suitable change of clothing. She pulled on jeans to protect her legs against the litter the tornado had left behind and got several pairs of long pants for Layla, too. They did not own suitcases since they'd never traveled, so she stuffed what daily necessities she could into pillowcases, laced up her running shoes and rejoined her boss.

"Okay. I'm ready." She had a plump pillowcase sack slung over each shoulder as she turned full circle for his perusal. "Does my outfit suit the occasion now?"

"Better than mine does."

"I was going to mention that," she quipped. "Well, now what? I suppose I should go to the church where all the other homeless people will be."

His eyebrows arched and he looked thoughtful. "You know, I do have one other suite finished in my building. If you'd like to live there for a little while, it's fine with me."

"*Live* with you?"

That made him laugh. "No. Not *with* me. As my neighbor. I'd been planning to renovate that entire second floor and eventually turn it into separate apartments. I took the corner suite but there is one other down the hall that fronts Main. It's clean and un-occupied. I've been using it for storage but it won't take long to move my extra stuff out and get you settled."

"I don't know what to say."

"Yes would be the logical answer," he told her.

Maya grinned. "Then, yes, as long as the rent isn't too high." The ensuing hurt that colored his expression surprised her, since she knew how frugal he usually was in regard to all his investments.

"I wasn't looking for a paying tenant. I was offering you a place to stay."

"I'm sorry." She felt the color rise in her cheeks. "I just assumed…"

"Well, don't," he said flatly. "You may think you know me a lot better than you really do. There are more important things in life than making money."

Blinking, Maya made a comical face in the hopes it would raise his spirits. "Wow. I think I should write that down for posterity. A Garrison actually saying that money doesn't count." Happily, she noted a slight smile begin to twitch at the corners of his mouth.

"Just don't spread it around, okay?" he replied. "I wouldn't want to ruin my family's image."

Maya laughed. "It's a deal."

"Is there anything else you want to bring with you right now?"

She shook her head as she looked at what was left of her cozy living room and kitchen. "Not that I can think of. I suppose we'll need some basic furniture but that can wait. I think the best thing to do is head for the office and see what we can salvage there, or go help at church."

"And leave your clothes in the apartment?"

"Yes." She knew he was simply being gallant but the notion of living under the same roof as her boss was off-putting, to say the least. Still, the apartment would be warm and dry—and free. There was no good reason to refuse his magnanimous offer, nor was there likely to be a better option anywhere else in High Plains, given the condition of many of the homes she'd seen so far.

Her mind insisted that she praise and thank God for this current opportunity and she did manage to do so.

Her heart, however, had serious reservations.

One of the elderly neighbors Maya had intended to check on stood on her own littered front porch two doors away and waved a greeting as they passed. "Yoo-hoo!"

"Hello! Are you all right, Miss Linda?" Maya called back.

"Fine. Just fine. Too bad about your lovely house."

"It'll be all right," Maya answered. "Keep an eye on what's left of it for me, will you?"

"Sure thing, dear. I'd ask you and Layla to stay with me but I'm going to be full up. My daughter's place over on Fourth was leveled and she and the kids are coming here."

"Are they okay?"

"Just fine, praise the Lord."

"I have been. All afternoon," Maya replied. She waved again. "You take care, Miss Linda. Best not go out till they get more of the wires and things picked up."

"I won't. You be careful, too. Especially with that pretty little girl." She grinned until her apple cheeks glowed before she added, "Nice to see you've got a big, strong man to look after you for a change."

Maya heard her boss begin to chuckle. She whipped around and gave him the sternest look she could muster. "Don't go getting ideas, Mr. Garrison. I may be letting you provide me with a place to stay for a week or so but I'm still capable of taking care of myself."

"I never said you weren't."

He continued to laugh softly, further aggravating her, so she decided to change the subject and focus on another of her gray-haired neighbor's comments. "God was certainly with us, and many others, this afternoon."

"How do you figure?" he asked.

"We're here, we're in one piece, and as far as we know so far, there weren't any serious injuries. If this had happened when school was in session or during that big Fourth of July celebration we held in the park last week, no telling how many people would have been hurt or even killed."

"I hadn't thought of it that way," he answered. "Guess we were pretty lucky in spite of everything."

"Luck has nothing to do with it. Like Miss Linda said, God was good."

"I don't know how you can believe in a God that would allow the chaos and destruction that's all around us."

All Maya said was, "How can I *not* believe when we're both alive and standing here having this conversation?"

Chapter Five

By the time they reached Main Street again, a young fireman in a heavy-looking yellow turnout coat and helmet was standing in the middle of the intersection and directing what little traffic was inching by.

"You can't go back in there," he shouted as they approached the office door. "The whole town is off-limits till we get it checked out."

Maya recognized the firefighter and hailed him. "Hi, Stan. It's me."

"Oh, hi, Maya. Sorry. I have my orders." He wiped perspiration from his brow with the back of his hand.

"We just came out of there, Stan. It was

fine, honest. All we want to do is drop off a few things and then leave again."

"Well…"

Though he never actually gave her permission, he did turn his back to yell at someone else. Maya took immediate advantage of the tacit opportunity and slipped inside with Greg and Layla.

The child was awestruck. "Wow, Mommy. Your office is really messy, just like my school."

"Only because of the storm," Maya said. "I pick up my things every day, and so should you." She heard her boss's low, soft laugh and saw his shoulders shake.

"That's what Miss Josie and Miss Nicki always say."

"They're smart ladies."

"Uh-huh."

Gregory paused at the interior door that led upstairs. He set Layla on the bottom tier where there was no standing rainwater and looked to Maya. "Shall we?"

Nodding, she handed him the pillowcases and followed her daughter up the steps while her boss brought up the rear. Since she had only recently come to work for Garrison Investments, she hadn't yet seen what had been done to the second floor or how the apartments had been divided out of the available space.

When she topped the stairs and stepped into the wide hallway she paused, astonished. Hardwood floors shone, the ceilings were a bright white with intricately molded cornices accenting their outer edges, and a brass chandelier hung from the center of a medallion as big as her dinette table had been before the tornado had smashed it to smithereens.

"Wow! When you fix up a place, you really fix it up."

"Glad you approve." He smiled. "I'd show you my suite but I haven't finished folding my laundry."

"If there wasn't an impressionable child present I'd stick my tongue out and give you the noisy raspberry you deserve," Maya said, rolling her eyes.

Layla clapped her hands. "Ooh! I love raspberries."

"It's a different kind, not like the ones we eat," Maya told her as she cast a warning glance at her grinning boss. "Mr. Garrison and I were just joking around."

"Oh."

He led the way on down the hall to an unmarked mahogany door, then opened it and stood back. "This is the spare suite. As I said, I have some boxes and things stored here but I'll get everything moved out as soon as possible."

Hesitating, Maya had to force herself to step forward. Layla had no such qualms. She skipped into the apartment ahead of the adults as if she'd lived there all her life.

"Ooh, Mommy, look! There's a boat in the living room."

Maya was about to disagree with her when she entered and realized the child was right. "I like your decor, Mr. Garrison. It's very outdoorsy."

"I brought the kayak with me from Chicago. I used to row it on the lake and I thought I might get a chance to paddle on the river once I got settled here. Never seemed to find the time, though."

"That's a shame," Maya said. "You work too much, too hard. Everybody needs some fun."

"As you so aptly observed, we Garrisons have a strong work ethic."

"No argument there."

Walking to one of the tall, narrow windows that looked out onto Main, she caught her breath. "Oh, my. Everything looks even worse from up here. There isn't anything left of the old town hall but the foundation. If that part hadn't been built of limestone it would probably have blown away, too. What a shame." She sighed and shook her head. "I just remembered. We were supposed to be having a meeting there tonight."

"Guess you'll have to cancel. What was it for?"

"I'm on the planning committee for the Founders' Day Christmas Celebration. We hold that same program every year. You must remember it."

"Vaguely. I was never very involved in town festivities."

"But you came to that celebration, didn't you?" Now that she thought about it, she didn't recall having seen him around much. Of course, she was younger than her boss so they would have traveled in different social circles. And speaking of society, she was also not in the same league as the Garrisons. Not even close. None of the Logans were. That was the way it had been almost since the time of the community's founding and nothing had changed much in recent times.

"I went away to boarding school the semester after my mother died," he explained.

"Didn't you come home for the holidays?"

"Not if I could help it," he said flatly. "Enough about my childhood. Let's drop off your stuff and head for the church. I'm sure they need all the volunteers they can get."

As she followed him out the apartment door and down the stairs, she had to wonder about his early life. Had it really been as lonely as his tone had made it sound? She supposed it could have been. After all, having a rich father was no sure sign of happiness. If she'd learned anything by being a single parent, it was that as long as she provided for her daughter's basic needs and also loved her with all her heart, the child would thrive.

It would have been nice to be able to give Layla more extras, but this storm would have stolen most of them anyway. Thanks to the tornado, folks were going to have to pull together, to help each other, to share what little they had left with those less fortunate. In a way, that was not such a bad thing.

Greg was the first one out the door on the ground floor. He went straight to the fireman, got his attention and pointed across to the hardware store and adjoining lumber yard.

"I told my people to let folks get whatever they need from the store and that goes for police and fire, too," Greg said. "Your departments can just help themselves. I'll be at the community church if you have any questions or need me for anything."

"Gotcha. Thanks, man."

"Glad to help," Greg answered emphatically.

Maya was waiting for him at the curb. "I heard what you said. That was very nice of you."

"Thanks. The only thing I can't understand is why you keep acting so surprised. You had me pegged as a real ogre, didn't you?"

"I wouldn't go that far. Actually, I hardly know you."

"That's right. You don't." Greg hadn't meant to sound so gruff, but he was getting pretty tired of being treated as if he were the world's biggest miser. He didn't mind if his father carried that negative reputation but he wasn't like Dan. Not in the least. Sure, he was a savvy businessman. There was nothing wrong with that, as long as he was honest and didn't take unfair advantage of anyone.

As they passed the High Plains Bank and Trust, which had been founded by his and Michael's great-grandfather, he was relieved to note minimal damage. That was also true of the new town hall that sat between Second and Third Streets. Some of the hardiest citizens were beginning to congregate there, too.

The General Store, on across Third, hadn't been so fortunate. Neither had Grocery Town next door to it. Apparently, the tornado had hopped, skipped and danced through the business district just as it had the nearby neighborhoods, leveling some buildings and totally missing others.

He paused long enough to inquire if the professional rescuers working in the grocery store needed his help, then rejoined Maya and Layla. "They've got a handle on it. They say there were some minor injuries but nothing severe, as far as they can tell. The shoppers and employees ducked into the walk-in coolers in the back of the market to ride it out."

"That was smart."

"Very. I also asked about the beauty parlor." He pointed to a shattered front window and partially collapsed facade. "They all got out in one piece, too."

Maya arched her eyebrows. "Phew. To look at the place you'd think anybody inside would have been killed."

As they watched, an ambulance slowly, cautiously, inched along Main. "No sirens," Greg observed. "That's a good sign."

"I know. I can't imagine what it's like at

our little local hospital, though. It must be terribly crowded."

"Thankfully, we don't have to go there for treatment and find out," Greg said soberly. "How are you doing?"

"Fine. You were right about the shoes."

"I'm surprised you admit it."

That made her laugh. "It slipped out. Forget I said it, okay?"

"Okay." He guided her across the front lawn of the church, then followed her to the side door that led to the annex containing the preschool.

"I'm going to see if I can leave Layla here for a little while," Maya said. "I can be of a lot more help in the kitchen, or wherever, if I don't have to keep an eye on her, too."

"Good idea. I'll go find Michael and see what else he needs. If the generator isn't already here, tell the ladies I'll have power for them soon."

"Will do." She paused, then gifted him with the sweetest smile he'd ever seen. "And I take back everything I thought about you, Mr. Garrison. You're all right. Just like regular folks."

He returned her smile. "I assume that means I should be grateful."

"Very," Maya said, laughing quietly. "You have no idea."

The next few hours passed in a blur. Maya found plenty to do in spite of the crowd of women who had already made enough cold sandwiches to feed a small army. Some people were arriving in shock, weeping and lamenting their losses, while some praised God and went right to work helping others. Surprisingly, there was as much laughter among the women as there were tears.

That had been one of the biggest surprises for Maya. The joy in spite of everything. It was as if she and her fellow survivors were happy just to be alive, to have their families around them, to be gathered in God's house where they could openly rejoice and either shed tears of relief or whoops of delight without censure.

As she worked preparing the dining tables in the fellowship hall to accommodate the large numbers of evacuees they were expecting, Maya wondered how her boss was faring. The image of him, kneeling and hugging Tommy, kept popping into her mind. If she lived a hundred years she'd never forget that sight. The man had shocked her all the way to her toes.

Overcome by a strong urge to see him again, to know he was all right, she checked with the others in the kitchen, was assured that there was nothing else that needed to be done, then picked up a spare plastic bottle of drinking water and excused herself to go seek him out.

He wasn't easy to locate. Dozens of men were laboring outside the church, making sure that no one was trapped in the collapsed structures nearby and clearing the streets for emergency vehicles as best they could with their bare hands. She finally spotted his blue shirt among the other workers and hurried to him.

"Hey. How's it going?"

"Pretty good." He straightened, wiped perspiration from his face with his shirt-sleeve and quickly downed the bottle of water she'd handed him. "Thanks. Man, it's so hot out here I'd almost welcome another rainstorm. But we didn't find any victims here so that's good news."

"I'll say. Michael's planning a short praise service tomorrow. Will you come?"

"I suppose so," he answered. "Don't want to tarnish my bright and shiny do-gooder image when it's so new."

She was about to offer a wry comment when she looked toward the river and saw a small boy near the water. "Is that Tommy?"

Gregory frowned and shaded his eyes against the late afternoon glare. "Could be. I guess we should go see."

"I'll go. You stay here and keep working."

"We're about done. Even if that isn't Tommy, I think we'd better see what the kid's up to. He could get hurt down there."

When he wiped off his hands and held one out to her, Maya took it. She realized that letting her boss hold her hand like that was probably too bold, but under the circumstances she was going to do it. She needed to feel his firm yet gentle touch, to rely upon his strength just a little while longer. And if casual observers took it for more than it really was, well, too bad.

Together they approached the river. The small boy had his hands cupped around his mouth and was trying to holler "Charlie" so loudly his thin voice squeaked.

Maya stepped aside and approached on Tommy's left. Gregory came at him from the other side. As soon as the child realized he wasn't alone, he tried to bolt.

Gregory snagged him by the neck of his striped T-shirt. "Whoa. Hold it, champ. We're not going to hurt you."

"I ain't goin' home," Tommy shouted. "I'm gonna find Charlie."

"It's awfully dangerous, especially so close to the river," Maya told him. "Did Mr. and Mrs. Otis give you permission to come out here?"

His lack of response told her the answer. Lowering her voice and bending to look into his eyes, she spoke gently, reassuringly. "We have a little more time before dark. If you'll promise to be good and stay with the people at the church, Mr. Garrison and I will keep looking for Charlie until the sun sets. How's that?"

"No. I'm gonna find him."

"Not if you fall in the river, you're not," Gregory interjected, still holding him fast. "Besides, our legs are longer. We can cover more ground faster than you can. Give us a chance. Let us help you."

Tommy folded his arms across his chest and shook his head firmly. "Nope. I'm gonna do it."

"Hate to disappoint you, kid, but that's not going to happen, at least not until more of this mess is cleaned up, so let's quit wasting valuable time arguing when we could be looking for your dog."

Certain that the boy would fight, Maya stood ready to assist, to reason with him. However, instead of beating on the man's shoulders the way he had during the tornado, Tommy merely slipped one arm around Gregory's neck and permitted himself to be carried.

Flabbergasted, she fell into step behind them. The wonders of the day just kept getting stranger and stranger.

They caught up with Reverend Michael and his fourteen-year-old niece, Avery, in the church office.

Gregory knocked on the open door, then entered. "Got a job for you, cousin. My friend Tommy needs a place to wait while we go look for his pup. Can you oblige?"

"Sure," the pastor said. "Avery can watch him. She was wanting something useful to do, weren't you, honey?"

"Oh, sure." The aloof-acting girl tossed her head, swinging her long braids over her shoulders as she stared at Tommy without cracking a smile.

Maya's gaze jumped from the rebellious teen to Tommy and the similar expressions she saw on both their faces made her smile. Avery was about to get a good lesson in what it was like to deal with a rebellious child. The experience might actually do the girl some good, not to mention Tommy.

"We'll head west, along the river," Gregory said, passing Tommy to Avery while addressing Michael. "I don't have a flashlight so we'll have to be back here before dark."

"Fine. There are more rescue crews working in the residential neighborhoods now that they've finished checking most of the downtown businesses. Looks good, so far. Last I heard, they thought everyone was accounted for except Lexi and Chief Ridgeway."

"Maybe they're together," Greg suggested.

Michael shook his head. "Unfortunately, I doubt that."

"Well, don't worry about us. We'll be back ASAP."

Michael shook his cousin's hand as he considered Maya gravely. "Are you taking her along?"

"Yes."

"Okay. Be careful."

"We will."

She waited till they were outside and headed back through the park before she said, "You sure have a way with kids. Especially Tommy."

"I wouldn't go that far but I do know he's pretty scared," Gregory answered. "He mostly needs a firm hand and fair rules to follow."

"Is that the way you were brought up?"

He shook his head. "No. There wasn't

much that was fair or stable in the way I was raised."

Judging by his apparently grim mood and the way he'd averted his gaze as he spoke, she decided to refrain from commenting. The Garrisons had always had plenty of money. Evidently, that had not been nearly enough to ensure happiness.

Greg wondered why he'd spoken so openly to Maya about his upbringing. It was no one's business but his own and he seldom revealed even a glimmer of the way he'd felt back then. So why had he told her?

Probably because of the severe stress they were all under, he concluded. That kind of trauma had to have a strong effect on everything, including a person's emotional stability. Sure, he and the other men had laughed and joked as they'd worked on the cleanup around the old town hall and church, but truth to tell, the circumstances were still so unthinkable they were hard to fully comprehend. Greg figured it would be days, if not weeks, before the total extent of the damage was known.

"Where do you think we should start

looking?" he asked to take his mind off his personal reflections.

"I suppose over toward the old Waters cottages," Maya answered. "I think that was the way the dog was headed the last time we saw him. He could have holed up there."

"If he wasn't picked up and blown into the river."

"If that's the case he probably didn't make it," Maya added.

"Yeah." Greg knew she was right. He just wasn't willing to accept defeat. Not yet anyway.

As they proceeded along the sloping, grassy banks of the High Plains River, they had to detour around limbs, downed trees and fractured lumber and roofing from houses that had been ravaged. The farther west they went, however, the fewer signs of the storm's depredation they encountered.

"Michael had mentioned maybe using some of the old cabins over this way as temporary housing," Greg said. "And that plan looks workable. The biggest problem is finding Heather Waters and getting her permission to open them up. He's lost track of her."

"I think she's working for a Christian aid agency somewhere. Last I heard, she was heavily involved in that kind of philanthropy."

"Thanks. I'll tell Michael."

Maya pointed toward the bank of small, quaint cottages that had once been part of the popular riverfront resort. "Will you look at that? The windows were boarded up so they couldn't be blown out and the rest of the place looks almost untouched."

"Except for a little wind damage and needing a fresh coat of paint." Greg pointed to some debris. "And that."

"I think that's just normal camping trash, not from the storm. There haven't been any renters out here for more years than I can remember. I'm pretty sure teenagers have used the area as a rendezvous."

When he arched an eyebrow and looked at her she blushed. "Not me, okay. I managed to get into plenty of trouble right around home."

"You? In trouble?" Greg grinned. "I can't imagine that."

"And I'd just as soon you didn't try to,"

Maya replied. "Suffice it to say that my parents had fits with both me and Clay. Jesse was the only good kid in our family."

"He'll be all right," Greg assured her when his gaze met hers and he read her concern. "You'll be able to phone him soon or we'll get out that way tomorrow. I'll see to it. I promise."

"Like you promised we'd find Charlie?" She sighed and raked her bangs off her forehead with her fingers. "Some things are not within our capacity to control."

"I thought you were trusting God?"

"I am. I do. That doesn't mean I'm not worried about my brother and his family. Marie's just out of the hospital and the triplets are still in the neonatal unit up in Manhattan."

"Well, at least they're safe."

He was sorry he'd spoken so glibly when Maya frowned, shook her head and answered, "Only if this same storm didn't hit up there, too."

Chapter Six

Although Maya knew that her boss was doing his best to allay her worries about her brother, there was really nothing either of them could do for the present. They'd tried using cell phones repeatedly, with no result, so she figured they'd just have to wait for service to be restored. Even then, that was no guarantee her brother's ranch would have any phone service.

Wading through puddles and avoiding piles of weeds and soggy refuse, they called for the missing dog as they wandered among the abandoned cabins that sat beneath a grove of ancient cottonwoods. Tufts of their feathery seeds drifted on the wind that still blew slightly, almost making it seem as if it were snowing. Right then, Maya would have gladly traded the sultry heat for a touch of winter.

"Watch for nails in these loose boards," her companion said, indicating some warped, faded, grayish siding that lay on the ground. "They may not have come from this last storm but they're still dangerous."

"Yes, sir." She stifled a giggle. She didn't know why she seemed so prone to inane laughter, except that perhaps she was simply so overwrought that her senses were skewed.

"You don't have to salute, okay?" he teased.

"I didn't. But it is a good idea. You've been acting a lot like a drill sergeant."

"I have not."

"Okay. Have it your…" Startled, she broke off in mid-sentence and grabbed his forearm. "Shush. Quiet. Did you hear that?"

"What? Charlie?"

"No. I don't think it was a dog."

"Then what?"

"It almost sounded like a baby crying."

"That's impossible. Michael said there

were only two people missing and they're both adults."

"Still, I thought… There. Hear it?"

"Maybe." He started forward slowly and Maya followed, taking care to make as little noise as possible.

She froze. "Stop. Over that way. To the right of that last cottage—the one with the lopsided front steps. I think I see something moving through those trees."

Though he turned and followed her directions, she could tell that he thought she was imagining things. Maybe she was. Or maybe she'd been hearing the wind whistling through cracks in the old wooden buildings and had mistaken the sound for a human cry.

Maya bit her lower lip, mulling over that possibility. *No.* She was a mother. She knew what she was hearing. It was a little one in distress. It had to be.

Passing her boss and taking the lead, she hurried through the trees toward the source of the intermittent noise. She had to pause several times to listen, to get her bearings again, before she drew close enough to see a bit of pink knit cloth in the deeper shadows.

Afraid of what she might find, Maya tiptoed closer. As soon as she realized exactly what she was seeing, she called out, "Greg! Over here. It's a little girl!"

Hurrying closer, Maya fell to her knees directly in front of the unsteady, weeping toddler and reached out to gently take her arm, to cup her muddy cheek. "Oh, sweetie."

He was beside Maya in a heartbeat. "Is she okay?"

Gently brushing loose debris from a tiny, reddened face, Maya said, "I think so." Sticky mud clung to the child's eyes, apparently making it painful or difficult for her to open them, and she was rubbing them roughly with tight little fists.

Responding to Maya's gentle touch, the toddler began to whimper and reach out to her, clasping one of Maya's fingers and hanging on with surprising strength.

"Let's get her out of the woods into better light and see for sure that she's okay," he said.

"We don't have any water to wash her. We won't be able to tell much until we get rid of all this dirt."

"The river," he said as he cautiously scooped the child up in his arms, unmindful of the mud.

Maya stayed right beside him, cooing to the toddler and speaking as if she were her mother. "It's okay, sweetheart. We're here. You'll be fine. Don't cry."

He proceeded as far as the top edge of the slippery riverbank, then gently placed the young child on the grass and stripped down to his white T-shirt. "I'll go get my shirt wet and we can use it to wash her off a little before we carry her back to town. I don't want to move her any farther if she's actually badly injured."

Concerned, Maya was crouching over the curly-haired blond toddler. "I don't think she's hurt much at all. She's moving her arms and legs and rubbing her eyes. The mud seems to be what's bothering her the most."

In seconds, he'd returned with the dripping dress shirt and began to bathe the child's face, starting with her eyes. When she finally opened them and looked at Maya, she immediately puckered up and began to wail.

"Guess she knows I'm not her mother," Maya said. "I wish I were. She's beautiful, even under all that dirt."

"There's a cut on her forehead and her knee's a little scraped but I think she's okay otherwise. I could leave you here with her and go fetch paramedics from town but that could take a lot longer, especially since we don't know if there's a unit available. I think the best thing to do is carry her in before it gets dark and we're all stuck out here."

"I agree. If we can't find anybody to treat her at the church, we can clean her up there and take her on over to E.R. ourselves if we need to."

He tenderly, cautiously, lifted the child again and cradled her in spite of her kicking and sobbing. "Keep squeezing water and rinsing her eyes so they don't get scratched any worse than they already are," he said.

"Are you going to be able to manage her?"

That made him laugh. "I trained on Tommy. After that, I think I could carry a wildcat."

"Uh-oh. Tommy. I totally forgot to keep looking for his dog."

"If it had been nearby when all this squalling started I imagine it would have come on the run."

"You're probably right. I just wish we'd found Charlie, too."

"One marvel at a time, okay?" he said. "In case you haven't thought of it, the only reason we stumbled across this poor baby is because we were out here looking for that dog."

"I know," Maya said soberly.

"It has been quite an afternoon, hasn't it?"

She nodded. "And the day's not over. Work is going to continue all night, I'm sure."

"Probably. Last I heard, all the gas station pumps were down due to a lack of electricity and the authorities were trying to figure out how to apportion fuel for the rescue equipment, let alone the nonessentials."

"If it's not one thing, it's another," Maya observed. She smiled at the child in his arms. It had quieted some and was now mostly sniffling with an occasional catch like a muted sob.

"Well, this is one fortunate kid and that's

a fact," he said, picking up the pace as they approached the church grounds.

Maya was blinking back tears of relief and joy as she looked up at the white bell tower with the cross atop it and whispered a heart-felt, soul-deep "Amen. Thank You, Jesus."

"There's a triage area set up in a tent on the east lawn," Michael told Greg as soon as he saw what he was carrying. "Where did you find her?"

"Out by the old Waters cottages. I thought nobody was using them."

"They're not supposed to be," the pastor answered, falling into step beside the others. "I guess there could have been squatters out there. Those cabins are far enough from town that trespassers probably wouldn't have been noticed for quite a while."

"That was my first thought but I doubt it," Greg said. "Maya and I were hollering for Tommy's dog and we'd checked out the whole area. Nobody made a peep. Except for this little girl, that is."

Maya nodded. "I heard her crying."

"Praise the Lord you did," Michael said.

"I'll tell the incident commander what's going on and let him send a properly prepared search-and-rescue unit out there. No sense having civilians stumbling around in the dark and getting hurt when we have plenty of trained people to do the job right."

"I thought you said only adults were unaccounted for," Maya remarked, trotting to keep pace with the men. "Who do you think this little girl is? Does she look familiar?"

Michael glanced at the child's scratched, dingy face as he gently stroked her hair. "No. I don't place her. We have lots of toddlers in our congregation but this one is a stranger to me."

"Me, too," Maya said. "I haven't seen any little girls like her in Layla's preschool or day care, either. I suppose she could have been visiting the area with some tourists. It is summer and we did find her near the river."

"First things first," Greg said flatly. "We don't need to know her name in order to get treatment for her. Not in an emergency situation like this." He led the way into the open-sided tent and went straight to a doctor clad in a formerly white coat that had begun to look a lot like the spotted, torn clothing everyone else was wearing.

"She seems okay to us," Greg told the middle-aged man, "but we have no idea how she got so far out of town or who her parents are."

The doctor put his stethoscope to the child's chest and listened while Greg continued to cradle her. "Sounds okay. I don't want to touch her eyes without sterile solution to flush them out. Best thing to do is have her transported to the hospital."

As he spoke he was feeling the toddler's arms and legs and flexing the joints. "No pain in her limbs and just one little bump on her head. I'd say she's fine, considering. Still, the hospital is the right place for her." He glanced toward the back of the tent. "Unfortunately, we don't have an ambulance available."

"Would it be all right if I carried her over?" Greg asked.

The doctor nodded. "I don't see why not. You got her this far. The sooner we put her into a controlled medical environment, the better."

Greg looked to Maya. "Are you coming or do you want to stay here with your daughter?"

"Layla's in good hands. I'll go with you. You might need me."

He wasn't about to argue. Yes, he could care for the abandoned child himself, yet it was somehow comforting to have Maya by his side. Although that was an unusual response for him, he wasn't too surprised by it. They had all been through a terrible trauma and everyone's emotions were bound to be on edge. Even his.

He shouldered through the crowd and started off toward the local hospital, taking extra care to watch his step so he wouldn't trip and fall while carrying the little girl.

"Funny. I'm kind of glad there was no ambulance," he said, once he and Maya were in the clear. "It seems wrong to turn her over to strangers when no one even knows who she is."

"I'm sure they'll find out. If not tonight, then soon. She must have parents nearby." Her voice became a whisper as she added, "I just hope and pray they survived."

All Greg could say was, "Yeah. Me, too."

* * *

Leaving their foundling at the chaotic hospital was harder for both of them than Maya had thought it would be. She almost wept as a nurse accepted the child, made a few notes on a chart, then hurried away with her, headed for the pediatric ward.

Gregory thrust his hands into his pockets and shrugged. "Well, mission accomplished. What now?"

"I suppose we should go back to the church. I haven't had anything to eat since lunch and you probably haven't, either, have you?"

"I'm not hungry."

"You have to eat. We're going to need all the energy we can get in the next few days." Looking into his eyes she saw more than intelligence; she saw empathy. And pathos. They might have laughed together over trifles mere hours before, but that didn't mean he didn't comprehend the weight of what others were going through.

"All right," he finally said. "We'll go eat. I just hope we don't run into Tommy and have to tell him we came back without his dog."

"I don't suppose he'd be the least bit impressed to hear that we rescued a child instead."

"I seriously doubt it. He told me that mutt was his only friend."

"I was afraid of that. What're we going to do?"

"Hope the dog finds its way home, I guess."

Little else was said as they made their way back to the busy church grounds. Gregory held the door for Maya and followed her into the noisy, crowded fellowship hall.

She was astounded by the number of survivors gathered there—and more were arriving by the minute, far more than they'd seen over by the new town hall. These folks were mostly women and children, Maya noted. That figured. Lots of men were probably still working, still digging, still part of the initial efforts to restore order.

"I'm going to grab a sandwich and coffee and head out again," Gregory said. "No sense just sitting here when I can make myself useful."

"Okay. The food's over there and you can wash your hands in the kitchen."

She led the way to the dwindling stack of sandwiches and handed him a paper plate after he'd dried his hands. "I feel the same way about not wanting to stand around, but I have no idea what else I can do."

"Probably nothing tonight," he said as he took several half sandwiches and a handful of chips. "By tomorrow I'm sure things will be better organized. They might even have the power restored so they can pump enough water to reach the rest of the town." He looked around. "Are you going to sleep here or go back to the apartment?"

"These people will need what little bedding the church has collected. As soon as I'm sure there's nothing more I can do to help, I'll leave."

"Okay. When you get to the apartments, let yourself into mine and take whatever you need. It's not locked. There are extra pillows and blankets in the hall closet. You can pull the loose cushions off the sofa and take them to your place. I'll help you move your bedroom furniture tomorrow."

"Really, there's no need for all that."

He was adamant. "Yes, there is. There's

not a lot I can actually do, no matter how much I want to. Let me help you and Layla. Please? It'll make me feel much better."

Smiling, she nodded in assent. "All right. Since you put it that way…"

Apparently satisfied, he turned and walked away. Maya watched him go, thanking the Lord that Gregory Garrison had decided to hire her, considering their families' past differences.

Reverend Michael would surely say that the Lord worked in mysterious ways if she told him her story, but Maya didn't need anyone to reaffirm that. Her boss had stopped her from risking her life when she had panicked, had kept her safe from the worst of the storm and had provided a place for her and her daughter to live in its aftermath. There was no more to say.

She smiled to herself. Whether Gregory Garrison liked the idea or not, God was working through him to help the helpless and comfort the fatherless, just as scripture taught.

Someday soon, she vowed, her smile becoming a wide grin, she was going to tell him exactly that.

And in the meantime, she had to locate Tommy and explain to him that they hadn't found Charlie. It was not going to be easy.

Maya had assumed she'd have to leave the church grounds and go to the Otis house to find Tommy, but when she walked outside she was relieved to spot the boy nearby. He was engaged in earnest conversation with an elderly woman who was apparently preparing to rescue displaced pets.

"You gotta find Charlie," Tommy explained to the gray-haired woman. He held out his hand parallel to the ground. "He's this big. And he's black, mostly. Except for a little white."

"I'm sorry, dear," the pet rescuer said. "We haven't had any dog like that brought in yet. Be patient. It hasn't been very long. Maybe he'll show up soon."

Whirling, hiding his teary eyes, the boy came face-to-face with Maya. He immediately brightened. "Did you find him? Did ya?"

The din from workers, survivors and newly arrived heavy equipment made it difficult to hear normal levels of speech. She laid her hand lightly on Tommy's shoulder and bent over so they could converse without raising their voices before she said, "I'm sorry, honey. We looked really hard."

"Sure you did." His lower lip quivered and stuck out in a pout.

"We did. Honest. Mr. Garrison is going to keep looking while he helps clean up this mess," she said. "And I'll keep my eyes open on my way home." She straightened. "Shouldn't you be getting home, too?"

"It don't matter."

"It doesn't matter," Maya corrected.

"That's what I said."

She let the misunderstanding go and smiled. "Okay. Are Mr. and Mrs. Otis around here? I'd like to talk to them."

His glance darted from side to side, evidently searching the crowd. "You gonna tell on me?"

"I do think it's only fair for them to know where you are. They'll worry about you if you're missing, just like you worry about Charlie."

Her heart nearly broke when the boy said,

"Not like me and Charlie. We're buddies 'cause we wanna be. They let me live at their house 'cause they have to."

There was nothing Maya could say in response that she felt he'd comprehend. Tommy was far too young to understand why some kindhearted folks took in needy children like him. Yes, they were paid for their trouble, but no amount of money could get some people to do what Beth and Brandon Otis did so lovingly.

Maya patted his shoulder. "Tell me where Mr. and Mrs. Otis are?"

Begrudgingly, the boy pointed to a knot of adults gathered beneath what was left of one of the cottonwoods behind the church. "Over there."

"Thanks. You coming?"

"I guess."

Maya likened Tommy's attitude and bearing to that of someone going to the dentist for treatment of a bad toothache. He dragged his feet but accompanied her just the same. Maybe later she'd get the chance to explain the foster system to him and help him grasp the fact that his temporary parents were caring for him because they wanted to, not out of necessity.

Right now, tonight, she figured the poor kid had enough on his mind. After all, he was only six years old, his dog was missing and his world had once again been turned upside down. This was not the right time to try to reason with him. Finding Charlie was the most important thing. He truly needed that scruffy old dog.

As she escorted the boy to rejoin his foster parents, Maya vowed that she would continue to do all she could to bring Charlie home to his young, lonely master. In the back of her mind, however, there seemed little real hope of doing so.

Chapter Seven

If Maya hadn't needed to make her daughter comfortable she wouldn't have set foot in Gregory Garrison's apartment. Layla, however, deserved a bed, even if it was makeshift, and at least a pillow. They wouldn't need other bedding to cover them on such a hot summer night, but blankets and sheets would help pad the sofa cushions so Maya took some of those and a few small towels for her bathroom, too. Thankfully, they had washed up before leaving the church. Their part of town still didn't have running water, let alone electricity or gas to heat it.

"I don't wanna sleep on the floor, I wanna sleep in the boat," Layla whined as her mother changed into clean shorts and a tank top, then began to make up their pallets side by side near the open window to take advantage of whatever cool breezes happened to stir.

"Well, you can't and that's that."

"Pretty please?"

"No kind of please, pretty or not," Maya insisted. "It's bad enough that we're bothering Mr. Garrison this way without wrecking his things."

"I won't wreck the boat. I'll be real careful. Honest."

"No."

"But, Mama…"

Maya arched her eyebrows and gave her child the sternest look she could muster under the circumstances. It would do her well to remember that Layla still had to be taught manners, no matter how glad Maya was to have her there, alive and well. The urge to weep for joy and gladly give the little girl anything she asked for was so strong she had to continually fight it.

Although Maya had always pictured herself as a loving mother, she also knew that her daughter needed rules. All children did. That really was a big part of Tommy's problem. Being passed from one home to another had undoubtedly left the little boy terribly confused. She knew she would have been at his age. It had been hard enough losing her parents as a teenager. Going through that as a small child had to be one of the worst things imaginable.

Fighting tears of sympathy, Maya helped Layla disrobe, slipped a light cotton gown over her head, then drew her into a tight embrace and held her close. "I'm sorry, honey. Really I am. But I don't have any other choice. We can't go home. You saw how awful our house looks. And we need a place to live till we can fix everything. Mr. Garrison was very kind to let us stay here and I don't want to do anything that will make him change his mind."

"Mama, you're squishing me," Layla squeaked, wriggling to get free.

Before Maya could brush away her sparse tears, the girl noticed. "Aw, don't cry, Mama." She patted Maya's hand. "I didn't mean it. I'm sorry."

Maya swiped at her damp cheeks and

forced a smile. "It's not your fault. I'm just sad because we don't have a place to live and I can't take care of you the way I want to."

"Then I'll take care of you," Layla said enthusiastically. She patted the pillows on their makeshift beds. "Say your prayers like a good girl and go to sleep."

Touched, Maya stretched out, closed her eyes, folded her hands for a quick bedtime prayer, then pretended to nap beside the sweet child.

When she heard Layla's deep, restful breathing begin, she slipped away and went to the window to take one more look at her formerly lovely town. There were times, like now, when she had so much trouble accepting the recent devastation she just had to see it again to believe it had really happened.

Below, recently arrived, portable gas generators hummed, and workers continued to toil. Temporary lights, which had been set up in several locations along Main Street, cast eerie shadows on the broken remnants of familiar buildings and sent fingers of pale illumination into the apartment where Maya stood.

The cloud-filtered moonlight on the park

across the street made it look to her like a graveyard for broken, toppled trees. Their black, shadowy branches curled and grasped as if they were the claws of a ferocious, predatory beast, bent on destruction.

That's what the tornado had been, Maya concluded with a lump in her throat. It was a monster that had chewed up High Plains and spit out the pieces as it tore across the countryside.

And she was one of those pieces. She and her family and friends. Late word had come back across the river that the Logan ranch had been hit by a smaller tornado, as she'd feared, but that no one had been injured there. For that she was doubly thankful, although she still wanted to hear the whole story directly from Jesse—to hear his voice again—and the sooner the better.

Maya closed her eyes and leaned her forehead against the frame of the open window. "Dear Jesus. What am I going to do? What are any of us going to do?" she whispered.

There was no easy answer, nor was there a way to plan for the future, at least not this soon. Later, when all the assessments had been completed and the rubble carted off, they could start to rebuild. But how many citizens would want to stay? she wondered. How many would simply give up and move away?

That was a good question. One of many that would be answered in the coming days and weeks. High Plains was long past its prime, as were many old towns that had been bypassed by the federal highway system. Yet people had held on and had managed to establish a productive, well-balanced community that served both itself and the outlying homes and ranches.

Other than a few trips to visit her premature nieces in the hospital, there hadn't been many reasons for Maya to travel even as far as Manhattan recently. Except for the larger hospital and some department stores that the bigger city offered, everything she needed was either available in High Plains or could be ordered. Plus, Manhattan was a bustling college town and she hated to fight all the traffic.

Looking below, she contrasted the chaotic

street with its normal peace and quiet. More than structures were gone. The ambience of her beloved town had been erased as well. She was going to miss that even more than the picturesque buildings themselves.

Greg labored with the men till he was so spent he could barely stand. Thankfully, other crews and equipment kept arriving from outlying areas, some from as far away as Wichita and Topeka, so the local workers could start to slack off a bit.

The police had their hands full sorting legitimate relief arrivals from would-be profiteers and looters. Passing vehicles now bore official-looking entry permits taped to their windshields.

And then there were the news vans. If one more reporter stuck a microphone in his face and asked him how he felt to have had his home town practically leveled, he was not going to be responsible for his response. Even Michael was starting to sound testy and that almost never happened.

Yawning, Greg decided to head home for a short time. He knew all he needed was a nap, not a whole night's sleep, and he'd be ready to go again.

He grabbed a couple extra bottles of cold drinking water in case Maya had forgotten to take any, then headed for the Garrison building.

Main Street was in better shape than it had been, he noted, but still not clean enough to make driving safe. Since it was paved with brick it would probably have to be swept by hand to prevent the heavy equipment from breaking it up. That would definitely take a lot longer than using skip loaders and dump trucks would have.

In passing, it looked to Greg as if Grocery Town was salvageable and would probably be back in business soon, though its front windows were blown out. He wasn't so sure about the General Store next to the grocery or the pie shop that sat between the Garrison Building and the bank. The fact that both those larger edifices had survived so well while Elmira's little bakery and diner had been devastated amazed him. He would have thought, given the shelter of the other buildings, the smaller one would have been well protected.

There didn't seem to be any rhyme or reason behind the demolition he passed on his way home. The funnel cloud had behaved like a flat rock skipping across the waters of a placid lake. No one could possibly have predicted which businesses would survive and which would be smashed beyond repair.

Keeping his hand on the banister he slowly climbed the darkened stairway to his apartment. His feet felt as though they were made of lead and his legs ached. So did his head and just about every other part of him. He was in great physical shape but this day and night had demanded far more of him than normal.

Not wanting to take a chance he'd frighten Maya and her daughter if he knocked, though her door was ajar, Greg paused there just long enough to place the bottles of drinking water on the hallway floor where she'd notice them easily. He was turning away when she spoke.

"Hello."

He jumped and whirled, peering into the

dim light reflected up from the street. "Whoa."

"Sorry. I thought you saw me. Why were you sneaking around?"

"I wasn't. I was being quiet so I wouldn't scare you."

"And I scared you instead?"

He could hear humor in her voice and it cheered him in spite of his weariness. "Let's just say you startled me."

"That's all semantics. How fast is your heart beating?"

It was pounding, all right. He doubted that was totally due to being surprised. There was something exceptional about Maya Logan standing there in the semidarkness, speaking to him in hushed, intimate-sounding tones. Something that stood the hair at his nape on end and gave him shivers from head to toe.

"I'm lucky it's beating at all," Greg quipped to cover his true reaction. "I'm whipped." He noticed she was still fully dressed. "Haven't you been to bed?"

"Couldn't sleep," she replied. "Layla's out like a light, though. She's mad at me for not letting her make her bed in your kayak."

He chuckled quietly. "If you had let her she wouldn't have stayed in there for long. It's awfully cramped. It would be pretty hot on a night like this, too." He wiped his brow. "I'm spoiled. I miss my air-conditioning."

"I know what you mean. I keep thinking I'll turn on a fan or get a cold drink. Our pioneer ancestors would laugh if they could see us now."

"Did you check my refrigerator?" Greg asked.

"Of course not."

"Well, we should. It's probably held the cold pretty well but there may be a few things we need to throw out and others we need to either drink, like juice or milk, or take to the church where they can be put to good use."

"I didn't think of that."

He gestured toward his door. "After you, ma'am."

"I couldn't." Maya glanced back at her daughter and was surprised to see the shadow of the child sitting up.

"Did he say I could sleep in his boat?" Layla asked. "Did he?"

"Not exactly. But Mr. Garrison did offer us a drink of milk or juice. Would you like that?"

"Uh-huh!" The three-year-old was on her feet and jumping up and down in an instant.

"Then, yes," Maya told him with a smile. "We would love to raid your fridge. Lead on."

Maya made Layla sit on a tall stool at her boss's kitchen counter to sip her juice so she wouldn't accidentally spill any on the plush carpeting. Although she could tell Greg was exhausted, she was desperate to learn more about what the rescuers might have discovered after she'd left the church.

"The only big find, besides the baby you and I brought in, was the police chief and some woman," he said, yawning and covering his mouth after he'd handed her a big glass of orange juice.

"They finally found Colt Ridgeway? Where was he?"

"Stuck in the basement of a vet's office. They say he'd taken his dog there and one of the twisters—we were right about their being more than one—dropped part of the building on top of them. Rescuers were digging for animals to save when they found the chief."

"And Lexi?"

"Who's that, the woman?"

"Yes. Lexi's Colt's wife. I mean, ex-wife. She's the only veterinarian in town so that's who it had to be."

"Then I guess she must have been down there with him. They said they got everybody out. They saved his big brown Labrador retriever, too. That's why he'd stopped there in the first place. To get a cut on the dog stitched up."

"I imagine there will be a lot of that kind of thing that needs doing. I found Tommy talking to an older lady over by the church tonight. There were apparently a lot of pets like Charlie who were frightened or hurt during the storm and she was starting to collect them."

He nodded. "I saw her. She had quite a bunch of cages and stuff piled up on the lawn by the time I left. When I asked about Charlie, she said she was taking in any animals that were found and keeping them safe till they can be claimed. So far, it was only dogs."

"That's understandable. The cats are probably still hiding," Maya said. "I had a calico when I was a girl. It spent ninety percent of its time skulking under my bed and would claw my ankles when I got too close."

"Sounds like a fun pet."

"Not really." Maya smiled. "I much prefer dogs. Layla loves to play with the cattle dogs at Jesse's ranch when we visit him, especially the puppies. They herd her as if she were a lost calf."

"She kind of is, right now. We all are."

"Did they say when the phones would be up and working?" Maya asked between sips of juice.

"It's my understanding that we should have cell phone service by tomorrow." He peered at the lighted dial of his watch. "I mean today. I haven't checked for a while." He reached into his pocket and handed her a flip phone. "Here. Give it a try. You never know."

"Thanks." Punching in her elder brother's number, she was surprised to hear a connection being made. Her eyes widened and she smiled. "Hey! It's ringing."

"Great. You should sleep better after you talk to him."

"Jesse? It's me, Maya." She knew her voice had an edge to it but she couldn't help being excited and apprehensive when someone answered. "Is that you? Are you okay?"

She heard a deep sigh before he replied. "I'm fine, sis. How about you and Layla?"

"We're both good. What about the ranch?"

"We had some damage to the house, primarily the kitchen, but the barns are still standing and we didn't lose any calves," Jesse said. "All in all, it could have been much worse."

"Did you wait it out in the root cellar?"

"No. I didn't have to. I was in Manhattan with the triplets when the twister hit here."

"What about Marie? Was she with you?" The silence on the other end of the line made her wonder if they'd lost their connection.

Finally, her brother said, "Marie's left me,

Maya. I found her goodbye note with the rings I'd given her when I came in from doing my chores this morning."

"What? That can't be."

Jesse snorted. "Yeah. That's what I kept telling myself. But she did me one favor. I was so upset I had to get out of here, so I left to go visit the babies. Doing that may have saved my life. I'd like to think it did."

Maya gripped the little phone more tightly and cradled it with her other hand. "Oh, Jesse. I'm so sorry. I don't know what she could have been thinking. Maybe it's because her hormones are all upset after the birth and she'll eventually reconsider and come home."

"I hope so. At least I think I do. I'm so confused right now I hardly know what to feel. All I can picture is those three tiny babies without a mother. It's not fair."

"No, it isn't. Poor Marie was always like a fish out of water living here, though," Maya reminded him. "I know she tried to fit in but she never really did."

"I don't know what else I could have done. I gave her everything she asked for, even the diamond engagement ring that's been in our family for ages. She left that behind with her wedding band, so it couldn't have meant much to her after all. Maybe I spoiled her but that was the way she grew up and I thought…"

Maya heard his voice break. Her heart did the same. Dear, sweet Jesse. He'd waited until he was older, more mature, to choose a wife. It hadn't helped. Marie had apparently been charmed by his dashing cowboy image without realizing that a rancher worked hard from dawn to dusk every day. Maya had tried to befriend her sister-in-law, to draw her into her circle of friends in High Plains and in church. To her dismay, Marie had usually found an excuse to beg off rather than join her in whatever outing or get-together she'd planned.

"You and the little ones are going to be fine," Maya assured him. "And I'll help all I can after they come home. How are they doing? Have the doctors given you any more idea of when they'll be out of the neonatal ICU?"

Jesse cleared his throat. "No. Not really.

They did say they may move them to a closer hospital later, so I don't have so far to drive. I'm not sure."

"Good thing you're on the other side of the river," Maya said. "The main bridge is closed. I'd have to go way around if I wanted to come up there. I will, though, if you need me."

"Not now. You stay there. I've been trying to phone you but the lines are down. How's your place?"

"A bit worse off than yours, it sounds like. But I'll be fine, big brother. My new boss has promised to pitch in and help me clean up."

"Garrison?" he huffed. "Are you saying that a Garrison offered to do anything, especially for a Logan, without making a big profit? I'll believe it when I see it."

"Well, he did," she insisted, casting a quick smile at her host to reinforce her praise. "As a matter of fact, I'm using his phone right now. Like you said, the main lines are down and I lost my cell, so hang on to this number in case you need to reach me. Did it come through on your caller ID?"

"Yeah. Got it."

"Okay. Take care. I'll be praying for everything." As she bid him goodbye and broke the connection, she sobered and handed the phone back to her boss. "Poor Jesse. I can't believe it."

"What happened? Was the damage worse than we'd heard?"

"That hardly matters in view of everything else. His wife left him this morning. They have newborn triplets and she just up and deserted them all."

"Ah, so that's why you didn't tell him that half your house is lying in a pile in your yard."

"That's why. He has enough to worry about without adding my problems to it all."

She took another sip of juice while she mulled over what she'd just learned. "I suppose having premature triplets was too much for Marie to cope with all at once."

"It sure would be if they were mine." He leaned a hip against the countertop and folded his arms across his chest.

"It's not as if they'd planned to have three at once. It just happened."

"Still, that is a lot to accept."

It struck Maya as inappropriate to be discussing such an intimate family matter with her employer so she changed the subject. "In the morning I'd like to go back to my place and salvage what I can from my kitchen and pantry. We can't cook here yet but it shouldn't be long. I have an electric fry pan and a crockpot that will come in handy, assuming they didn't get picked up and flung into the next county."

"We'll take my SUV if we can't borrow a truck," he said. "I suspect the insurance adjuster will say your car is totaled."

Her eyes widened. "And yours isn't? They were parked practically next to each other."

"I know. Yours had a close encounter with a snapped telephone pole. It missed mine. All I need is a new windshield—and a few less dents in the hood."

"Terrific. What else?"

"Nothing that I can think of at the moment. My brain is as tired as the rest of me."

"And we're keeping you up. I'm sorry." She lifted Layla down from the stool and took her hand. "Thank you for your hospitality, Mr. Garrison."

"You'd better drop the formalities and start calling me *Greg,* the way you did when you got so excited and forgot yourself out at the Waters cottages." He gave her a lopsided grin. "After all, we are living under the same roof and even sharing a refrigerator."

Maya rolled her eyes and shook her head. "Don't remind me, okay? I have enough real problems to worry about right now without adding rumor and gossip to the list."

He laughed. "Okay. I've got a flashlight right here. You take it so you can see your way home. I won't need it tonight."

Their hands brushed briefly as she accepted the light. His touch was barely there, yet she shivered in response to the contact. Hoping he hadn't noticed, she backed away with a simple "Thanks."

"You're welcome. Good night, Maya."

Pausing at the door she turned, smiled and said, "Good night…Greg."

The scariest aspect of that small utterance was that it had felt good, felt right. In the space of a single day, she and Gregory

Garrison had apparently progressed from the formal relationship of boss and employee to that of friends. How unbelievable was *that?*

Chapter Eight

The following morning passed in a blur. Maya had used Gregory's—Greg's—phone to try to reach her other brother, Clay, after she'd dug her personal phone book out of the mess in her living room and had found his work number. Disappointingly, she'd been forced to leave a message for him. His boss had informed her that Clay was out in the Canadian wilderness, guiding a hunting party, and was therefore incommunicado.

Greg had made four trips with Maya to her house to pick up furniture and anything else she wanted to move. They were in his pock-marked SUV, stopping in front of the

Garrison building with their final load, when his cell phone rang.

He answered, spoke briefly, then turned off the motor as he held out the phone. "It's your brother."

"Clay? Already? They told me he wouldn't get my message for weeks."

"No. This is Jesse. He says it's urgent." Lowering his voice and covering the mouthpiece Greg added, "He sounds terrible."

Heart in her throat, Maya took the instrument. "Jesse? What's wrong?"

She waited while he struggled to speak. Finally, he blurted it out. "Marie's dead."

Maya was glad she was seated because she suddenly couldn't draw a breath. All her strength vanished. Her hands began to tremble. "What happened?"

"An accident. Chief Ridgeway just came by to tell me. Marie was driving and…and… a tree…"

"Take your time, Jesse."

She heard him cough to try to cover his raw emotions before he continued. "A tree was knocked over by the storm. As near as they can tell, Marie had pulled over to wait out the tornado and she was in the wrong place at the wrong time."

"They're sure it was her?"

"Positive. Somebody has to make an official identification, for the record. They can't tell by her wedding and engagement rings because she left them behind on the kitchen table, like I said, and the tornado blew everything away, but the chief says there's no doubt in his mind. It's her, all right."

"Oh, Jesse. I don't know what to say."

"Neither do I. And it gets worse. I still have to notify Marie's parents. I'm really dreading it."

"I can understand that. They never were very friendly to any of us." She paused, then mustered her courage and asked, "Do you want me to do it for you?"

"No. It's my job. Just say an extra prayer for me, okay? I've tried to reach them at home and all I get is an answering machine. I refuse to leave them a horrible message like that."

"Of course not. And if there's anything I can do, anything at all, just give a holler."

"Do you have your own cell phone yet? I tried your house again and the call didn't go through this time, either."

"Just keep using this number for a while. I'll get back to you when I locate my cell or buy a new one."

"Okay. Thanks for listening. I feel better just having talked to you, Maya. You always were the level-headed one."

"And you were the good one," she countered. "Mama always said so." She sighed slowly, deeply. "So, what's next?"

"I'm heading for the hospital. I just want to be with the babies. Right now, I hardly know if I'm coming or going."

"I wish I were there to give you a big hug."

"I can feel it over the phone," her brother said. "Tell—tell Reverend Michael to be ready to conduct a funeral soon."

Maya heard his breath catch in a muffled sob before he managed to bid her goodbye. She closed the phone and handed it back to Greg. Although he didn't ask, his inquisitive look prompted an explanation.

"Jesse's wife, Marie? The one who left him? She was killed by the tornado."

Greg's jaw gaped. He gently covered Maya's hand with his own. "I'm so sorry. I heard you ask if there was anything you could do but I thought you were just talking about the cleanup. Is there anything he needs? Any help we can give him?"

"He says not. I suppose there will be once he starts coming to grips with it and has to arrange her funeral. He wants me to alert Michael."

"I'll do that for you, if you want," Greg said.

"Thanks. I appreciate the offer but Jesse asked me to do it. Besides, Layla's in day care and I suddenly want to see her again. To give her a big hug and thank God she's okay." Maya managed a wan smile. "I suppose you think that's silly."

Greg started the car. "Not at all. I would have been surprised if you hadn't wanted to. There are some heartbreaking situations that only being with loved ones can fix."

As he drove, Maya mulled over his comment and wondered who he yearned to be with during trying times. Judging by what she'd observed in the past few days, Gregory

Garrison felt and acted as if he were totally alone in the world.

That conclusion made her almost as sad as hearing about her brother's loss.

Michael was in the church basement with his niece, Avery, and a group of other young people, sorting donated clothing and bedding, when Maya and Greg arrived.

"Sorry to bother you," Greg said, leaning in the doorway and addressing his comments to his cousin. "Maya just got some bad news and she needs to speak with you." He eyed the teenagers who were obviously listening to every word with interest. "Privately."

"Of course." Michael excused himself and joined Maya and Greg in the hallway. "What is it? What's wrong?"

"It's Jesse's wife," Maya said haltingly, softly. "She was killed in the storm."

"Oh, no."

"I thought maybe Chief Ridgeway had told you already."

"No," the pastor said, "I haven't seen Colt since last night when I visited him in the hospital. I didn't even know he'd been released."

"He was out at Jesse's ranch this morning, bringing him the bad news. Jesse was terribly upset. I'm so worried about him."

"That's not at all surprising." Michael glanced back at the teams of youth working to sort disaster relief supplies. "I'll drive up there to counsel him as soon as I can get free."

"Don't worry about it right now," Maya said. "Jesse's going to the hospital in Manhattan to see his daughters. He wouldn't be home if you did go to the ranch. He just wanted me to ask you to preach at Marie's funeral."

"Tomorrow's Sunday. Perhaps I'll see him in the morning, as usual. If not, I can make arrangements to drive out his way in a day or so and we can discuss what kind of service he would like."

"I was really hoping he would come to High Plains for church, even if he has to go way around to get here," Maya said. "I think it would do him good to be with his church family at a time like this."

"So do I," the pastor replied. "But we should let Jesse make that choice. Not everyone grieves in the same way. He may not be ready to accept too many condolences, no matter how sincere they are."

Greg was watching Maya's expression and was relatively certain when she made the decision to refrain from elaborating on her brother's marital problems.

Her lips pressed into a thin line and she scowled. "There's a bit more to it than what I've told you, Reverend Michael. You'll need to speak to Jesse in person."

Michael took her hand. "All right. I'll get in touch with him as soon as possible."

Greg could see unshed tears in Maya's pretty brown eyes. She stepped back. "If you'll excuse me, I really need to go see my daughter right now."

Greg watched her hurry down the hallway, her shoulders square, her spine stiff. "It must be really tough to try to raise a kid all by yourself," he said.

"Yes. But she's doing a fine job."

"I agree. You heard about her house?"

"Not in detail." Leaning against the wall, the

pastor folded his arms across his chest and looked questioningly at Greg. "How bad is it?"

"Pretty bad. We managed to salvage the bedroom furniture and a few little things from the kitchen but half the house is a total wreck."

"*We?* As in, you and Maya?"

"Yes," Greg answered with a half smile. "We. I had an extra apartment available in my building and we moved her and Layla into it this morning. They were lucky their beds and dressers were usable because I don't know how long it will be before her place is livable again." His cousin looked far too pleased to suit him so he added, "*What?*"

"Nothing, nothing. I'm just surprised, that's all."

"Not half as surprised as I was," Greg said. "One minute I was working in my office and everything was normal, and the next I was up to my neck in rain and rubble and practically adopting my secretary and her little girl."

"Life can be interesting, can't it?"

Greg arched an eyebrow as he studied

Michael's expression. "Don't look at me like that. I'm just doing my civic duty."

"Right. Which reminds me, thanks for the generator. I don't know what we'd have done without it."

"You're welcome. Do you have enough gas to keep it running till the power comes back on?"

"Uh-huh. Emergency services brought us some, and one of the insurance companies has a tanker standing by if we need more. They also brought in portable bathrooms and cases of drinking water."

"With what ulterior motive?"

Michael chuckled and clapped Greg on the back. "Cynic. I could ask the same about you and Ms. Logan."

"Whoa. Back off, Mike. It's not like that. She needed a place to stay and I had an extra, empty suite down the hall. That's all there is to it."

"Right. It's strictly business. You don't even like her. Is that what you're saying?"

Greg chose to stop and think before answering too quickly. He did like Maya. And her daughter. Beyond that, there was his admiration for the woman's spunk and intelligence, not to mention the fact that when she wasn't wearing suits and high heels, she looked far more approachable.

"Let's just say we've become friends," Greg finally said. "The storm has probably brought out the best in her."

"And in you, cousin," Michael said with a broad grin. "I didn't think I'd ever see you pitching in the way you have or offering to give away stock from your stores. I'm impressed."

"That wasn't why I did it."

"I know." Michael thumped him on the back again as he started back into the room where his teenage crew was still working. "And that impressed me even more. You're a real blessing, Greg. To all of us."

Left alone in the hallway, Greg just stood there, deep in thought. Him? A blessing? Hardly. He'd worked all his life to earn his father's approval and had not succeeded. How anyone could see him as a blessing in any respect was beyond him. He was just a regular guy, doing what he could in a bad situation. Anyone would have done the same.

As he started down the hall toward the day care to rejoin Maya, he began to wonder if that was true. Was he unique? He doubted it. Maya Logan, however, was definitely one of a kind and he was almost glad they'd gone through the tornado together.

He'd had to think twice about hiring her in the first place, in view of their families' history of conflict. If subsequent events had not occurred the way they had, he might never have gotten to know her as a person. A mother. A neighbor.

He began to smile as he added one more definition. *Friend.*

Maya knew the instant Greg opened the door to the day care room. She sensed his presence even before their eyes met.

Tommy jumped up and greeted him eagerly. "Did you find my dog? Did you find Charlie?"

"No. Sorry." He ruffled the boy's hair. "But don't give up hope, okay. I just talked to the lady outside collecting lost pets. I reminded her what Charlie looks like and that he's still lost, in case somebody brings him to her."

"Yeah, sure." The child turned away, sulking.

Maya motioned to Greg and called, "Tommy was helping us make a new sign for the door. Could you come over here and spell the words for him?"

"Sure." Greg shepherded the disappointed child in the right direction. Sizing up the diminutive chairs and deciding they might not support him, he chose to get down on his knees at the table. "Okay, Tommy. What do you need?"

"Nothin'. I can do it myself."

"I'm sure you can. But Ms. Logan asked me to help, and I always listen to her."

She rolled her eyes theatrically and muffled a chuckle. Greg might not realize it, but he was a natural at handling children now that he'd loosened up a bit. He could switch from being a hardheaded businessman to thinking on Tommy's level in a heartbeat and make perfect sense to the six-year-old. That was more than a lot of adults could do.

Tommy didn't look up but he did say, "Okay."

As the two worked with their heads bent over the cardboard sign and shared markers to color in the letters, she was so touched by Greg's empathy for the little boy she nearly wept. That man would make a great father someday. Someone patient and kind, like him, was exactly what Tommy needed.

Cleaning up the office enough to get by hadn't been as hard as Maya had anticipated. They'd swept up the broken glass and had placed most of the wet papers in cardboard boxes to sort through them later. Then, she and Greg had moved the desks to one side to allow him to rip out the sodden carpet.

She held the broken door for him while he struggled to drag the last carpet strips out onto the sidewalk. They were clearly a lot heavier wet than dry and he was sweating profusely.

"Are you sure I can't help you?"

"Just keep the door open and stay out of the way."

"Okay, okay. I'm on your side, remember?"

"I know. I just can't believe this mess."

"I can't believe how fast we're getting it cleaned up."

"You must be joking."

Maya grinned over at him. She'd donned jeans and an old T-shirt for the dirty work and was also perspiring, so she'd tied a cotton bandanna around her forehead. "Not at all. Look on the bright side. We don't have to do this upstairs, too."

"No, but there is still your house to consider."

"I told you. We can't touch any more there until the insurance people take pictures of the damaged areas. Besides, I don't think there's much else left over there to save."

"You're probably right about that," Greg said, wiping his hands on his jeans and coming back inside. "What do you want to do about living-room furniture?"

"Honestly? I hadn't even thought about it. There are too many other things on my mind."

"We could take a run up to Manhattan and shop for a sofa or something."

"Now? Don't be silly. I'll just take a few lawn chairs upstairs and sit in those. Why buy new furniture? I'll probably need every cent I can scrounge or save to rebuild my house. It's going to be expensive. Everything is these days."

"True. But there are ways to cut corners, especially if you know the guy who owns the lumber yard."

Maya didn't reply. She desperately wanted to restore her house to the way it had been, but she was already too in debt to her boss to suit her. If he did much more for her she was going to feel so beholden to him it would ruin their working relationship.

Sobering and sorting through the stack of damp files on her desk, she fought her emotional reactions—tried to reason them away. Greg had helped her, yes, but she wasn't the only one, nor was he her only possible source of aid. The church deacons would have provided for her, had she chosen to ask. She knew that for a fact. She also knew that others in High Plains had far greater needs than hers. It was those people who should come first.

So, what shall I do, Father? she prayed silently. *Shall I take Greg's charity or refuse? And if I do that, where will I live and how will I care for Layla?*

Maya didn't need a voice from Heaven to answer her questions. It was obvious that the Lord had already provided for her and her daughter. She had a job, a place to live and a bright future in spite of everything. All she had to do was swallow her pride and accept it.

Sneaking a sidelong glance at Greg she was surprised at how her heart swelled and began to pound. The always perfect, always overly neat man looked so different in his worn jeans and sweaty shirt she could hardly believe the transformation.

And it wasn't merely his clothing, she added, half chagrined, half in awe. The change extended all the way from his short hair and sneaker-clad feet to the tender soul she'd glimpsed when he'd ministered to Tommy with such empathy. Like it or not, she was enamored of the man. The only question remaining was how long she'd be able to continue to work for him—and with him—when her emotions were so far out of whack.

Chapter Nine

Singing along with the rest of the congregation at the impromptu praise service that evening, Maya looked around the packed sanctuary. Beth and Brandon Otis were there, as usual, accompanied by a sullen Tommy. Many others of her neighbors had come, too.

There were also nearly as many strangers present as there were regular parishioners. Most looked as if they had come in straight from working on the cleanup, which was no problem to a church like High Plains Community. They accepted everyone, rich, poor and anything in between. If a person wanted to worship the Lord, he or she was always welcome, regardless of circumstances.

"Please bow with me in prayer," Michael said as soon as the song ended.

He thanked God for their survival and the chance for the church to assist those in need, before launching into praise that all present were well enough to attend in spite of the disaster.

As soon as Maya folded her hands and closed her eyes she pictured Greg. It was always thoughts of Greg that filled her quietest times. She had quit arguing against his being one of the primary instruments God was using to help her, and for that alone she gave special thanks. He had put a roof over her head, given her unquestioning support and had even kept his promise to attend Reverend Garrison's special service.

Yes, he and the young pastor were cousins. And, yes, he had chosen to sit with some of the other men instead of next to her, but Maya didn't care. Greg was here. In a house of worship. That was all she needed to start believing that he was on his way to reviving his latent faith. How could it be otherwise when he had already seen so many blessings come out of the aftermath of the storm?

Beside her, Layla fidgeted and tugged on the hem of her cotton blouse. "Mama?"

"Shush."

"But, Mama…"

"Not now."

Maya sat down and took the child's hand as soon as Michael said *Amen*. "Okay, what?" she whispered.

"Can I go to the nursery with Miss Josie?"

"I don't think she's here tonight. Her grandma's in the hospital and she's probably visiting her," Maya replied. "Just sit here with me for a few minutes and then we'll eat supper in the fellowship hall with everybody else."

Listening to Michael's litany of praises and special needs, Maya was pleased to hear that Josie's grandmother's injuries were not life-threatening and that the police chief had escaped with only a few bruises and a cracked bone in his arm.

"We're also blessed to have heard from Heather Waters about the cottages down by the river," Michael said. "She's going to allow us to use them for temporary housing as long as necessary. If you need a place to stay, see me after the service and we'll add your name to our list for possible place-ment."

He continued with the usual litany of folks who were feeling poorly for other reasons and who also needed uplifting.

When he concluded by mentioning Jesse's name and explaining about Marie's acciden-tal death, tears clouded Maya's vision. She was having great difficulty accepting the fact that Marie was gone forever and she couldn't imagine that Jesse was doing any better, es-pecially since he'd spoken with Marie's parents. They had all met accidentally while visiting the triplets in the hospital and it was then that Jesse had learned why they were in the area. They'd come to rescue Marie from her unhappy marriage. From her life with *him*.

In the end, Jesse had reluctantly given them permission to take their daughter's body home for burial after it was released by the coroner, which meant there would be no funeral service for Marie in High Plains, no family grave in the old churchyard cemetery. And therefore, no real closure for poor Jesse.

Dear Lord, help my brother, she prayed. *And tell me what to do, what to say to him.*

She had already decided to post Marie's picture outside the church and encourage folks to leave flowers and mementos there as a memorial. Beyond that, she didn't know what to do.

"Where is Clay when we need him?" she asked God in a hushed whisper as soon as Michael was through speaking and began to dismiss the congregation for dinner in the fellowship hall.

Close behind her, she heard a deep, familiar male voice say softly, "I thought you'd talked to Clay."

She whipped around, startled to see Greg. "No. He's still out in the wilderness somewhere. All I could do was leave a message." Her eyes narrowed. "Hey, weren't you sitting over on the other side?"

"Yes. I didn't see you when I came in."

"No wonder, as crowded as it is," Maya said. "Will you come along and eat with us?"

"Are you sure? We don't want to start rumors, remember?"

Blushing, she answered aside. "I'm afraid it's too late for that. Several people have asked why we were holding hands down by the river yesterday. Then there's Miss Linda's opinion that I'd finally found a nice man, too. All in all, there's already plenty of talk going around."

"Hmm. Sorry."

"Don't worry about it. I'm a big girl. And I've had to deal with plenty of gossip before."

"Well, at least you and I know there's nothing wrong going on. Everybody else should know better, too."

Maya managed a smile and silently thanked God once again for that man. It had taken her years to live down her unwed mother status and accept the fact that there would always be a few townspeople who looked down on her because of it. Now, here stood the formerly stuffy, formerly difficult-to-please Gregory Garrison, telling her that he had no doubts about her character. And he clearly meant every word.

That realization brought fresh tears to her eyes.

To Greg's surprise, the other parishioners slapped him on the back, shook his hand and generally treated him as if he were a regular member of their church family. He figured that was probably because Maya was introducing him to everyone in the fellowship hall and he was also carrying Layla, but it felt good nonetheless. So good, in fact, that he happily instructed everyone to call him Greg instead of Gregory or Mr. Garrison, just as he had Maya.

"Everybody's so friendly," he said to her. "No wonder Mike loves it here."

She smiled up at him as she began to fill a plate for herself and one for her daughter. "Mike? I've never heard anyone else call him anything but Michael."

"I guess I still think of him as my rotten little cousin, Mikey," Greg said, grinning. "He was into everything. It was my job to make him behave whenever we were together because I am five years older."

"It's hard to imagine my pastor as a naughty little boy." Maya was dishing up potato salad. "Are you sure I can't fill a plate for you while I'm at it?"

"No. Just take care of the princess and yourself. I'll get something later, after you're both settled."

Hearing herself referred to that way made Layla giggle, as he had intended. Children were resilient. Still, all this upheaval had to be hard on them, especially those who couldn't go back home. He knew it was odd timing that he'd had the second apartment finished just when it was going to be most needed, but he was far from ready to give credit for that foresight to a higher power. He was simply the kind of man who liked efficiency and it had been logical to have the work done while a seasoned crew was available.

Which reminded him. Finding a carpentry team that was both trustworthy and able to take on the job of fixing Maya's house was going to be tough, considering the state of many buildings in town. Above all, they'd have to be very careful to avoid hiring one of the fly-by-night operations that were circling High Plains like vultures.

Greg followed her to a table and placed the little girl in a folding chair beside her mother as he asked, "Have you heard anything more from the insurance company?"

"Nothing definite. An adjuster did tell me that if my house had been leveled, the way the town hall was, I'd get a settlement check sooner. As it is, there will have to be a full inspection, a cost analysis, and maybe even an engineer's report done before they can give me more than the money to cover replacement of my house's contents. And since I only lost half of that…"

"Terrific. How long did they say all that paperwork would take?"

"From a couple of weeks to several months. Maybe longer."

Noting her apologetic expression and raised eyebrows, Greg was sorry he'd pressed her. "Hey. Don't sweat the small stuff—and it's all small stuff when you look at the bigger picture. You can stay in the apartment as long as you need to."

"I know. But I am going to pay you something for rent. I wouldn't feel right living there if you don't let me do that."

"Okay. How's a dollar a week sound?"

"Don't be silly."

He couldn't help noticing how cute she looked when she was making silly faces at him. Greg laughed. "Okay. You drive a hard bargain. Make it two dollars, but that's my final offer."

When he noticed her eyes growing misty he stepped away and changed the subject. "Well, if you two are all set, I'll go get myself something to eat before the good dishes are gone. Save me a seat?"

"Of course," Maya said as she laid a napkin on the chair beside her to mark it as taken. "Hurry back."

That was a given, he mused, a bit surprised at his eagerness to rejoin her. Nothing in his life had been the same since the tornado. He craved orderliness, sameness, a future that was planned and executed with skill. That was the way he had always lived and that was the way he intended to conduct himself in the future. Yet here he was, trapped in the midst of chaos—and he felt happier, more needed, than he had in his entire life.

Maya could not drive anywhere until her car was repaired or replaced. High Plains was a small enough town that walking wherever she wanted to go was not difficult. She missed her car mostly because it had had air-conditioning and the July heat was sweltering, especially since the storm had raised the humidity. Even the nights retained the oppressive heat.

It was twilight when she, Greg and Layla left the church together and strolled home through the park. Thankfully, a breeze was blowing off the river and that brought some relief.

"Phew," Maya said, sighing and facing into the wind as she raked her bangs off her damp forehead. "That's better. I don't remember a summer this hot since I was little."

"Probably because you've gotten used to air-conditioning," he replied. "Like you said, we're spoiled."

"True. I used to think we were as capable and tough as the folks who settled High Plains, but I'm changing my mind about that. They had to be extraordinary people."

"They were. And it's not just the Kansas summers they had to cope with. Can you imagine having to raise your own food and prepare everything from scratch?"

Maya rolled her eyes. "No. But if Grocery Town doesn't reopen soon we may all find out what that was like."

Chuckling, Greg pointed to that closed market on the opposite side of Main. "I saw activity in there this afternoon so I stopped to talk to the guys doing the cleanup. They think they can have the place back in working order in a few more days. Their biggest problem is power for the coolers and freezers, but even without that they can still sell fresh food and canned goods."

"That's a relief."

"Why? Don't you like peanut butter sandwiches?"

Layla was quick to answer, "I do!"

When Maya looked into his eyes she saw a teasing twinkle that made her laugh. "I used to. They're getting a little boring lately. I was so glad to have a hot meal at church tonight, I think I'd have eaten just about anything."

"We did. What was that brown stuff in the crockpot?"

"I don't know. Stuffing, I guess. It had to have come out of a box. Those church ladies are amazing. I think they could keep an army fed if they had to."

"They are feeding an army," Greg answered. "I can't believe how many outsiders have showed up already, and I know it's just the beginning. If we were a functioning town we'd make a fortune from all the tourists and extra workers."

"Now you sound like the old Greg Garrison."

"Do I? Sorry. We can use all the help we can get. Which reminds me. I stopped and asked Michael if there was anything else he needed and he signed me up to go help open and clean the Waters cottages. That's what I get for volunteering, huh?"

She could tell that, in spite of his protestations and occasional reversion to his former frugality, Greg was eager to pitch in and lend a hand. It was as if he had a new lease on life, a new outlook that had made him seem happier than she'd ever seen him.

"Have you found out if the Garrison homestead is all right?"

"Yeah. It's fine. Dad and his nurse took cover in the springhouse, just the way the old-timers used to, and the ranch hands hunkered down in Nora's old storm cellar behind the house."

"I had forgotten all about that spring-house. Even if they don't have electricity out there, your father can probably keep his perishables from spoiling if he puts them down there, can't he?"

"Not as well as modern refrigeration would but, yes, he can, as long as the spring keeps running through it." He smiled wistfully. "I used to hide down there and dangle my bare feet in the icy water when I was a kid like Tommy. It was a good place to go to escape doing chores, too. It was always cool, even in weather like this."

"Makes me want to visit," Maya said.

"Not me. I'd rather roast than pay any extra visits out there."

"I'm sorry you feel that way," she said quietly, sympathetically. "I'd give almost anything if I could see my mom and dad again."

"If you believe everything Michael says, you will."

That brought a tender smile and she looked directly at Greg, meeting the obvious challenge. "I do and I will," Maya said with clear assurance. "But that doesn't mean I don't miss them every single day."

They had entered the stripped office building and were heading for the stairs leading to the apartments above when the overhead lights flickered.

Greg stopped. Waited. Started to grin when the lights came on and burned steadily. "We have power!"

"And air?"

He laughed at her eagerness to be cooler. "Let's let them get the whole grid up and running before we ask too much of it, okay? I'd rather have a refrigerator than air-conditioning."

She pulled a face. "Well…"

"Come on. I want to go check how much of the building is functional and whether there was any damage to the circuits. We don't want the power on if there's a short somewhere in here."

Following him up the stairs with Layla,

Maya asked, "Is there anything you just take at face value? Or do you always insist on double-checking every tiny detail?"

"I check. Doesn't everybody?"

"No," she said with a quiet laugh. "You are one of a kind."

"You say that as if it's bad."

"Not really, I guess. I'm just not used to being around a person who picks at every little thing the way you do."

"You've never known anybody else who's like that?"

"Only one person," she answered, sobering. "Layla's father."

Greg turned at the top of the stairs to study her expression. In a way, she seemed to want to tell him about her past. Was she waiting for him to ask? Maybe. Or maybe it was the last thing she wanted to talk about. There was only one way to find out.

"I don't know who the guy was—and I'm not asking you to tell me his name," Greg said, "but he had to be a fool to leave you and that sweet little girl."

"Thanks." Blinking and averting her gaze, Maya appeared to be avoiding the subject.

"Forget I mentioned it," he said quickly. "It's none of my business."

"I guess I don't mind telling you if you really want to know," Maya said, speaking softly and looking up at him. "I suppose I'd rather you hear the story from me than as distorted gossip."

He stood very still, waiting, giving her time to organize her thoughts and decide how much, if anything, to reveal.

"I was engaged to be married but I was having my doubts even before I found out…" She glanced at her daughter as the child skipped happily off down the hall. "You know."

"I get the idea."

"When I told my fiancé what had happened he was furious. I actually thought he was going to hit me when I refused to consider terminating the pregnancy."

Greg's jaw clenched. "That's inexcusable."

"I probably would have come to my senses and broken our engagement, if he hadn't suddenly left town and saved me the trouble. I have no idea where he went."

"Have you tried to find him?"

"I did at first. Then it occurred to me that a life without him was a blessing. I don't need his help to raise our daughter. As a matter of fact, it's best that he's out of the picture so Layla never has to deal with him. He had a terrible temper."

So, that was what had kept her single all this time, Greg mused. He'd wondered why an attractive, available woman like Maya Logan had never married. Now, he knew. She'd not only been disappointed by love, she'd been emotionally scarred by a man in whom she'd once placed her trust. A man who wasn't worthy to shine her shoes.

The forlorn look in Maya's eyes spurred him to offer advice in the form of a question. "Have you talked with Michael about what happened?"

"No. I wasn't a member of his church until after Layla was born and I didn't want to have to explain the situation all over again." She hesitated. "It was hard enough telling you just now."

"Maybe you should reconsider opening up to Michael. I'm no theologian, but is it possible that God was sparing you by sending that guy away, protecting you and your little girl from a life of abuse?" Judging by the way her jaw dropped, she had never before considered that possibility.

"No," Maya said after a short pause. "I wasn't stuck in the relationship. I could have walked away any time I'd wanted to."

"How about after Layla was born? What if her father had stayed right here in town so you couldn't escape him? Suppose his temper had led to even worse violence? How would you have protected her?"

"I—I don't know."

"Then I've made my point," Greg said. He took the lead and started down the hallway. "I'll check your place first and make sure it's safe, then we can all turn in. Since you don't have a refrigerator yet you can keep using mine for as long as you need to."

"Maybe we can dig my fridge out tomorrow and test it to see if it's okay after we photograph it for the insurance company. It didn't look like it was in too bad a shape when we picked up the bedroom furniture. I don't care if it's dented, just as long as it works."

"We'll do that in the evening, after I'm finished working on the cabins," Greg told her. "By then, the streets should be in better shape for driving. I don't know why I haven't had a flat tire already."

"Maybe the Lord was watching out for us."

Chapter Ten

Although Sunday was supposed to be a day of rest, you sure couldn't tell it this particular Sunday, Maya thought.

Of course, there was the scripture about pulling your sheep out of a ditch even if it happened to fall in and get stuck on the Sabbath, so she figured this situation wasn't all that different. Thankfully, more outside help was arriving by the hour to relieve the weary locals.

She had already posted Marie's picture outside the church and had left flowers below it herself, although she'd had to beg some of her neighbors for what little was left of their usually lush gardens in order to come up with enough for a pretty bouquet.

Maya was glad to see that the sanctuary was crammed to the aisles when she stepped inside for the worship service. That figured. Facing their own mortality and surviving, the way they all had, was a surefire method of increasing the size of a congregation. Too bad the positive effects would probably be short-lived.

Maya had planned to invite Greg to accompany her to Sunday services but he'd apparently been up and gone by the time she'd knocked on his door a little after eight because he hadn't answered.

She had been thrilled to discover that there was hot water for a shower, probably thanks to his customary attention to detail—the same meticulousness she had once thought of as a character flaw.

Picturing Greg's reaction to that kind of criticism made her smile. As far as he was concerned, his methods were the only right way to do things and he wasn't shy about saying so.

It was that degree of confidence that had

made him so successful in business. It was also the biggest stumbling block to letting herself care for him romantically. Taking orders at work was one thing, but in her personal life was totally different. And totally unacceptable. She'd managed to muddle through as a single parent thus far and she would continue to do so for as long as it took to guide Layla successfully into adulthood.

The sight of Greg approaching via the maroon-carpeted center aisle of the sanctuary banished all negative thoughts. He looked wonderful. And terribly pleased to see her, too.

She grinned and scooted over to make room for him. "Good morning."

"Morning. Where's our princess?"

"In the children's service," Maya said, choosing to ignore his casual reference to Layla belonging to both of them. "I was afraid she'd get too restless and bother other people, especially since it's so crowded this morning."

She paused and fidgeted as she tried to ignore the warmth she sensed from his closeness. What was the matter with her? She no sooner got through assuring herself that she could not possibly care for this particular man than he walked in and once again took her breath away. The lingering trauma of the tornado had obviously unhinged her.

Michael led them all in his customary opening prayer before the choir director announced the first hymn. Maya was chagrined to note that she and Greg were going to have to share a hymnal. As she opened and held it out, his warm, strong hand covered hers and she could barely read the words, let alone sing with her usual confidence and joy.

Greg, on the other hand, had a beautifully rich baritone. The sound of his singing sent shivers along her spine and made the fine hairs on her arms prickle.

Dear God, she prayed silently, *help! What's wrong with me?*

No divine answer was necessary. She knew exactly what was wrong. She was making the terrible mistake of falling for her boss, yet she had no idea how to stop what was happening or return to the uncomplicated, impersonal relationship they had shared just a short time ago.

The only saving grace, as far as Maya was concerned, was that Greg was unaware of her burgeoning feelings for him. Heaven help her—literally—if he ever suspected.

The second song went no better. By then he had not only covered her left hand, he had turned slightly and begun to stand even closer, as if they were the only two people present. At least that was how it felt to Maya. They were merely sharing a hymnal, yet they were doing it as a couple, not as individuals, and she was awed by the sense of perfect companionship that gave her.

As the singing concluded, Greg closed the book and bent closer to whisper, "Are you okay?"

"Fine. Why?"

"No reason."

The pastor began to speak, drawing her back into the worship service. She had nearly regained her composure when Greg reached over and took her hand.

She knew she should pull away. She would. In a minute or two. After all, Greg wasn't used to coming to church and she didn't want him to feel unwelcome.

If you really believe that's why you're letting him hold your hand, Maya told herself, *you're even further gone than you thought you were.*

And now he's got me talking to myself, too, she added, perplexed and flustered. *Next thing I know, I'll be giving his hand an affectionate squeeze.*

As if on cue, her fingers contracted ever so slightly and she did just that.

Greg's response was to smile at her and gently tighten his grip.

Head swimming, heart pounding, Maya wondered if she was ever going to regain her self-control or if she was destined to spend the rest of her life on an emotional roller coaster. She consciously hoped not, but truth to tell, she was secretly wondering what surprises were still in store.

Michael's sermon was as much a history lesson as anything else. He contrasted the faith of the Old Testament patriarchs with that of the founders of High Plains, including Will and Emmeline Logan, who were Maya's ancestors, and Zeb and Nora Garrison, who were Greg's.

He concluded with a reference beginning in Isaiah 55:8. "I can't tell any of you why disasters occur or why extraordinarily damaging tornadoes have hit High Plains. I can only quote the prophet Isaiah. 'For my thoughts are not your thoughts, neither are your ways my ways, saith the Lord. For as the Heavens are higher than the earth, so are my ways higher than your ways and my thoughts than your thoughts.'"

Michael paused, then continued. "I can't begin to know the mind of God. None of us can. But I do know He has given us a chance to reach out to each other and show that His spirit is living in each of us."

Greg once again squeezed Maya's hand as Michael concluded in prayer.

By this time she was beyond pulling away. On the contrary, it was beginning to feel so right to have him holding her hand that she was loath to think of the moment when he would finally release her and they would go their separate ways.

* * *

"I've been wondering how our little friend is doing," Greg said as they headed for the child care room to pick up Layla after the service.

"Who? Tommy? The last time I saw him he was hanging around the lady collecting stray animals."

"That figures. I'm concerned about him, too, but I meant the little blond girl we found. Have you heard anything about her?"

"No. And she has been on my mind. Do you want to walk over to the hospital and visit her?"

He shrugged. "Think they'd let us in?"

"I can't see why not. After all, we found her in the first place."

"Assuming anyone remembers us. It was pretty hectic Friday night."

"That's putting it mildly," Maya replied. "It's all kind of a blur."

"I know what you mean."

"You do?"

Greg chuckled and nodded. "I sure do. Until I finally got a few hours sleep last night I hardly knew if I was coming or going."

"You were doing both," she teased.

"How right you are."

When they opened the door to the room full of children, Layla immediately squealed in delight and ran straight to Greg. Surprised and flattered, he swung her in an arc and carried her out while Maya followed, looking a bit chagrined. He could understand that. She'd been Layla's only caretaker for so long it must be hard to accept the fact that the child was fond of someone else, too. The astounding thing was that the little girl seemed to genuinely like him. *Him.*

He chose to make light of it for Maya's sake. "I think the princess likes the view from way up here. That's what you get for being shorter."

"My feet reach the ground so I must be tall enough," she quipped back. "That's what my brothers always used to tell me. They both inherited Dad's height. I'm more like my mother was."

"I imagine you wrapped both Clay and Jesse around your little finger just the same. I never had siblings but I can picture you lording it over those bigger, older boys."

"I might have. Just a little." Maya smiled wistfully as she looked at Greg. "I really miss Clay."

"Where did you say he was?"

"Being a real cowboy, as usual, up in the wilds of Canada. He's guiding pack trains for hunters so he's out of touch with civilization for weeks at a time. Sometimes longer. I keep telling myself that's why he hasn't called me back. I doubt there's any way he's heard about what the tornadoes did here."

"You weren't specific when you left the message for him?"

"No. I didn't want to scare him to death."

"He'll call eventually. He's a Logan so he's probably good and stubborn, but he'll phone you when he can. I know he will."

"What do you mean, Logans are stubborn? I'm not."

It was all Greg could do to keep from bursting out laughing. He settled for a knowing grin. "Of course you're not. You were eager to listen to my advice when I told you we needed to go to the basement during the storm and you couldn't wait to accept my help afterward. Right?" His grin widened when she made a silly face.

"Okay, okay. You've made your point."

"Good." As he led the way out of the departing crowd and started across the church lawn, Tommy Jacobs ran up and tugged on the back of his jacket.

"Did you find Charlie?" the boy demanded. "Did ya? Huh?"

"Sorry, no," Greg said. "But I'll be going out again this afternoon to work by the river and I promise I'll keep my eyes open for him while I'm there." As the child's countenance fell and he started to walk away, Greg asked, "How's it going at home? How are your foster parents doing since the storm?"

"Okay, I guess." He worried the muddy grass with the toe of his already dirty sneaker. "Mrs. Otis stays in bed a lot but Mr. Otis is a pretty good cook—if you like hot dogs all the time."

"Is she sick?"

Tommy shrugged. "I dunno. Nobody talks to me."

"Well, I'll keep looking for Charlie," Greg assured him. "Don't give up hope, okay?"

"Yeah, sure."

All Greg said as the boy left them was, "Poor kid."

"Should we go look for Charlie now?" Maya asked.

"Not if we plan to go very far. Like I said, I promised Michael I'd help him do more work on the Waters cottages this afternoon and I only have about an hour free. That's enough time for a meal. Are you hungry?"

"Where do you propose we go? The pizza place is still closed."

"Yes, but Isabella's is open."

"That's so fancy." He saw her glance down at her casual outfit and flat shoes.

"I'd be delighted to take you there—or anywhere—even if you were wearing shorts and old tennis shoes," Greg said. "Don't be a snob." The instant he'd said that he rued being so frank.

"Me? A snob? No way."

At this point he saw no graceful way to recant so he forged ahead. "In reverse," he explained. "You're assuming that just because the prices are higher at Isabella's Ristorante, the people inside are stuck up and wouldn't accept you. I've been dining there often since I came back to High Plains and I happen to know that's not so. They're just as down to earth as you and I are."

She arched a graceful brow. "As I am, maybe. There is nothing down to earth about you."

"Ouch." He pretended to grimace to cover the fact that her comment had truly wounded him. "I thought, after the past few days, you were beginning to see me as a real human being."

"I am. I do. But you can't change the fact that you're a Garrison, any more than I can change being a Logan. As Reverend Michael reminded us this morning, we come from very different backgrounds. Your people were rich mill owners and merchants and mine were dirt-poor cattle ranchers."

"So?"

"So, that's just how it is."

"No," Greg countered, "that's how it *used* to be. We've come a long way since then. Don't get so focused on the past that you miss out on the future, Maya."

She didn't say another word until they got

to the hospital, and even then she directed her comments to others, rather than to him. If he hadn't been carrying Layla he wondered if her mother would have even acknowledged that he was still there. It pained him to imagine that she might not have.

Blond, petite, Nicki Appleton was leaving the hospital as Maya and the others arrived. She greeted everyone with a smile, centering its brightest glow on Layla. "Hi. How's my favorite pupil doing?"

"We're all fine," Maya answered over her daughter's squeal of delight. "What brings you here, Nicki? Is everything okay?"

The preschool teacher nodded. "It will be. I've been visiting that poor, lost little girl you found out by the Waters cabins."

"Do they know who she is yet?"

"No. We've been calling her Kasey. The initials *K* and *C* were embroidered on her shirt so it seemed natural to put them together like that. We tried every name beginning with a *K* sound that we could think of and she didn't respond to any of them."

"Will they let us see her?"

"I can't see why not. Maybe Layla being there will encourage her to talk more. The area where you found her was searched thoroughly and there was no sign of her parents or anything that may have belonged to her or them. We're stuck unless she identifies herself."

"What will happen to her?" Maya asked, deeply concerned.

"As soon as she's released I'll take her home with me," Nicki answered. "I've fostered babies before and since she can also go to work with me, it won't pose a hardship."

"That sounds ideal. Which room is she in?"

Nicki pointed, gave brief directions, then bid them goodbye and hurried off.

As Maya entered the hospital and made her way down the hall, she knew that Greg was following close behind. She could feel his presence and hear Layla babbling to him in her childish way. To his credit, his replies were always given as if he and the child were having an intelligent, adult discussion. He never patronized or talked down to her, nor did he seem to be holding a grudge since Maya had fallen silent.

Truthfully, she hadn't known how to respond to his suggestion that she was clinging to the past. Her first reaction had been to categorically deny it. Then, as she'd begun to mull it over, she'd decided he might have a valid point.

That, of course, was not something she intended to tell him.

Greg could *not* be as good as he seemed, she argued. No man was. She was merely overwrought at present and would soon be back to her normal, logical, sane self. She just hoped she didn't slip and do something rash before that happened.

Like what? she asked herself.

Her cheeks flamed the instant her heart answered far too honestly. *Like kiss him the way I've wanted to. And hope he kisses me back.*

Her steps momentarily faltered.

Greg touched her elbow. "What's wrong?"

"Nothing," Maya answered, disgusted. "I'm just so mad at myself I could scream."

"That's probably not a good idea in here," he teased. "You might end up in their psych ward."

Hearing the amusement in his voice she whipped around, hands fisted on her hips, and faced him. "Well, if I did it would be your fault, you, you…"

Well, that was certainly an adult response, Maya concluded, so upset she could hardly think straight. *And totally befuddling, if the look on Greg's face was any indication.*

She clenched her teeth to stop herself from continuing past the point of no return.

Layla had already had her arm around the man's neck. Now, she leaned closer to whisper in his ear.

As Maya watched them, she saw a grin spread across his handsome face. His dark eyes sparkled and there were little smile lines at the corners—lines she was becoming all too familiar with.

"What?" she demanded. "Are you two conspiring against me now?"

"Not at all," Greg said. "The princess was just assuring me that you might sound mad

but you didn't mean to." His smile widened.
"Is she right?"

With a grimace Maya did the only fair
thing. She answered honestly. "Yes."

Chapter Eleven

The curly-haired blond toddler was napping in a crib when Maya, Layla and Greg entered her hospital room.

"She looks so tiny," Greg said softly.

Layla seemed fascinated but also held tightly to him. "Who is she?" the three-year-old asked.

"We don't know. Your mother and I found her after the tornado and brought her here."

"Where's her mama?"

"We don't know," Maya replied. "They can't find her."

"She looks sad."

Greg gave Layla a little hug as he continued to carry her. "She'll be okay. The doctors and nurses will take good care of her here."

Once again, Layla leaned close to his ear to speak only to him.

This time, instead of sharing her comments, he excused himself. "We're going to go back to the lobby for a second. Wait for us here?"

Maya nodded. She had approached the bed and was gently stroking the child's hair away from the small bandage covering the injury to her forehead.

Seeing Maya's kindhearted ministrations touched Greg's heart and made his gut clench in a way that was unfamiliar to him.

As he and Layla hurried away, he was thankful for the break. Staying so near to Maya of late had been doing strange things to his thought processes. He knew he'd done the right thing when he'd offered her the spare apartment, yet he was beginning to have serious misgivings about her being so close by all the time. Working with her was one thing. Having her as his neighbor, being with her constantly, was clearly another.

Greg entered the gift shop and set Layla

down. "Okay. Your choice. Pick a toy that you think the little girl would like. Just remember she's younger than you are."

Taking her assignment so seriously it almost made him chuckle, Layla wandered among the stuffed animals as if her decision was critical. She picked up one toy after another, weighed it carefully, then moved on.

He glanced at his watch. "Tell you what. Choose any one now. In a few days, if Kasey hasn't gone home with Miss Nicki, we'll come back and buy her another toy. Okay?"

"Okay." Layla handed him a small pink teddy bear similar to the ruined one he'd seen Maya pull from the rubble of her living room.

He passed it to the clerk, asking quietly, "Do you happen to have two of these?"

"Yes," she whispered. "Would you like them wrapped?"

"Not this one," he replied with a wink. "We'll take this upstairs with us now. Charge me for two and wrap the other one. I'll pick it up in a few minutes on my way out."

"Yes, sir." She removed the tags, then bent

and handed the bear to Layla. "Here you go, honey. I hope your little friend likes it."

Greg paid quickly and followed Layla to the elevator. Judging by the affectionate way the child was hugging the gift bear, getting a second one had been a good decision. The fact that she hadn't asked for anything for herself made him doubly glad he'd bought two.

Kasey was awake by the time they rejoined Maya at her bedside. She seemed a bit shy until Layla approached and offered her the stuffed toy. Greg saw their gazes meet and sensed a childish empathy.

"See? She likes it," he told Layla. "You made a wonderful choice."

"Uh-huh." The child's expression was one of both joy and subsequent sadness as Kasey cuddled the small pink bear and began to babble to it happily.

"Have you been able to get her to talk well enough to tell what she means?" he asked Maya.

"No. She's said plenty but nothing I could make sense of. Layla was speaking in short sentences when she was about this age. I'd hoped for the same."

"Maybe she'll do better once she's out of a hospital setting. She's certainly happy with her new toy."

"I know. Layla used to have…"

Standing off to the side where the three-year-old couldn't see his face, he placed a finger across his lips to silence Maya and gave her a nod toward the door. "I have to be back to work with Mike soon and we haven't eaten yet. I think it's time we headed for Isabella's."

"Okay." Although she took her daughter's hand and started toward the door, she looked puzzled.

As soon as they reached the hospital lobby, Greg gave her a sign to wait and ducked back into the gift shop. When he emerged carrying a gaily wrapped gift and handed it to Layla, he thought Maya was going to cry.

"She seemed to love it and there were two just alike so…" He knew he was grinning foolishly but the little girl was so thrilled with the simple gift he couldn't help himself. She tore away the paper and hugged the bear as if she were greeting a long lost friend.

Maya picked up the discarded wrapping and wadded it into a ball. "You shouldn't have."

"Yes, I should," Greg countered. "She didn't ask for anything for herself. All she was concerned about was buying the perfect toy for Kasey and I figured she deserved one of her own."

"That was so sweet."

To his surprise his cheeks warmed. "Hey, that's me," he joked to cover his embarrassment. "Mister Nice Guy."

"Well…"

Her slow drawl, misty eyes and lopsided smile made him laugh softly. "Okay, okay. I won't press it. Wouldn't want to undermine my reputation as a ruthless businessman."

"I'll keep that in mind," Maya said. Her smile became one of adoration as she cast a loving look at her child. "But I won't ever forget what you just did, either." Her subsequent "Thank you" was delivered with a catch in her voice.

Greg didn't know what to say in reply. He had done it for the little girl, not to impress her mother, yet it seemed he had pleased them both.

If he'd been sure it was wise to be glad about having done that, he'd have felt a whole lot better about the situation. Unfortunately, he was having serious misgivings in regard to almost everything that had to do with Maya Logan. He already liked her far too much for his own good, and his emotional attachment to her and her daughter was increasing so rapidly he could hardly keep track of his burgeoning feelings from moment to moment. This was not good. Not good at all.

For Maya, remaining near Greg was beginning to be as necessary as breathing. She craved his presence, his strength, his wit, and even his sage advice, although she was loath to admit the latter, even to herself. What was wrong with her? They hardly knew each other. If it hadn't been for the way the tornado had disrupted everyone's life, they might never have progressed past being employer and employee—barely acquainted and hardly friends.

And now? The sight of his handsome face and his adorable expression as he had presented the teddy bear to Layla was permanently etched in her memory. She hadn't been exaggerating when she'd said she'd never forget that kindness. She was positive it would stay with her the rest of her life, just as other special events had.

And speaking of special events, she reminded herself as she took a last forkful of lasagna, they needed to reschedule the committee meeting regarding the Founders' Day Christmas Celebration. No matter how impossible or inconsequential it seemed today, December would be here before they knew it and everyone would expect life to have returned to normal by then.

Finished eating, Greg laid aside his napkin and leaned across the narrow restaurant table to ask, "What's wrong? You look worried all of a sudden."

"I was just remembering the Founders' Day planning that never got done. We'll need to rebuild the town hall from the ground up. And I'm not sure how many committee members will be available, even if I wait awhile to reschedule everything."

"So, start with plans to rebuild. You said

you'd have gotten a quick settlement if your house had been leveled. The same should be true of the town hall."

"I hadn't thought of that. I suppose we will get some money soon. Trouble is, I have no experience in construction so I have no clue how long it might take to build a replacement." She paused, thoughtful. "I know we'd want it to be just like the original."

"It could look the same," Greg said, "but you'll have to use modern materials in order to bring it up to code, especially since it's a public building."

"Oh. What a shame."

"Not entirely. It will be a lot less likely to accidentally catch fire like that house over on Third Street did after the power came back on. Today's wiring and breaker boxes are much safer than those old fuses were. You could also put an interior safe room or storm cellar in the plans if you wanted to."

"I don't know. Maybe. That old building stood firm in all kinds of weather for more than a hundred and fifty years. I'd have to see what the rest of the committee think about making changes."

"Who's on it besides you?"

"The city council and Mayor Dawson, of course. And Reverend Michael and I. We do most of the organizing with the help of Glenis Appleton, Nicki's mother. My brother Jesse drops in whenever he can get away from the Circle L. The same goes for Chief Ridgeway. He shows up when he's not on duty. We can always use more steady, dependable members. How about joining us?"

Greg recoiled and raised his hands, palms out, as if she'd just suggested something sinister. "Whoa. Not me. I'd end up making everybody mad the minute I opened my mouth."

"Only if you insisted that your ideas were the only right ones." She waited for his wry grin to appear and wasn't disappointed.

"Suppose they are."

"Suppose they're not."

His grin widened. "Now you're hurting my feelings, lady. When have I been wrong? Name one time."

Sobering, Maya said, "When you offered me a free place to stay."

"I was doing you a favor. How was that wrong?"

She looked into his dark eyes, willing him to understand and not take offense or over-react when she said, "I don't know how you feel about it, but I'm having far too good a time when we're together. And in case you haven't noticed, we're together a lot."

"Is that so bad?"

"It's not bad at all," Maya said softly. "It's good. That's the problem." She cast a sidelong glance at her daughter. "I don't want—us—to become too attached to you. It wouldn't be fair."

"Why? Because I'm not your type? Or because you still hold it against me that my family is well-to-do?"

"No," she said, shaking her head and lowering her eyes to the linen napkin she had clenched in her lap. "Because you told me when you hired me that you'd be leaving High Plains as soon as your father passed on."

"Suppose I change my mind?" Greg asked.

"Have you?"

"I might."

"And you might not," Maya said, getting to her feet and easing Layla's chair back as he rose on the opposite side of the table. "Thank you for a lovely meal. When you see Michael, tell him I'll get in touch about the planning meeting."

In one way, Maya was sorry she'd been so blunt. In her deepest heart, however, she knew she'd done the right thing by speaking out. Even if Greg wasn't becoming as attached to her and Layla as they were to him, her reasoning made perfect sense. The child had never had a father to love her. And it had been a long, long time since Maya had felt anything this strong, this compelling, drawing her to any man. The last thing any of them needed at a trying time like this was to have to come to grips with unrequited love.

That thought seared her all the way to her core. *Love? Oh, yes.* In the space of a few days she had fallen head over heels for her boss. And if he didn't stop doing things that touched her heart and made her love him even more, she was going to have to look for a different place to live.

The way she saw the touchy situation, she was tempting fate if she remained his neighbor. He had already made it a practice to touch her hand. Sooner or later they might even share a kiss. That would be terrible. And wonderful.

Would God have thrown her and Greg into such close proximity if He had not planned for them to fall in love? she wondered. Or was this a test of her faith, her determination to be a good Christian in spite of trying circumstances?

She didn't have a clue. And with her pastor busy helping others and also working with Greg on the Waters cabins, there was no way to catch Reverend Michael and confer with him in private. At least not right now.

Therefore, Maya decided, she'd go back to her old neighborhood and see if she could assist her neighbors. And she'd visit the remaining half of her home, too. Maybe there, in familiar rooms that had once afforded such comfort, she could reason through her dilemma regarding Greg. It was worth a try. Anything was better than stewing over her emotions.

Or over one immovable force, she added wryly. Gregory Garrison had a mind like a brick and he was twice as hardheaded.

"And I'm no smarter," she muttered. "If I were, I would have refused the apartment the minute he offered it."

Would she have? Probably not, she concluded. Even in retrospect she could see that she had been attracted to Greg all along. She may not have realized it, but the beginnings of those feelings had been brewing from the moment she had stepped through the office door to apply for the position as his executive assistant.

Accepting that fact made Maya even more furious. She was an adult. A mother. The sole supporter of her only child. Surely she had accepted that job for her daughter's sake.

Yes, but you always thought he was handsome, she added honestly, *even if you didn't think you'd ever be romantically attracted to him.*

Maya felt as if she were arguing with an intractable foe when, in truth, she was pitted against only one. Herself. How in the world could she expect to win *that* battle?

* * *

Michael put Greg and the other men to work taking the boards off the cottage windows and checking for leaks in the roofs. Surprisingly, the old cabins had weathered the storm with little damage. They had been sealed up for years, so mostly needed cleaning, although more would have to be done to them eventually.

"We'll have at least five of these ready by this afternoon," Michael said, wiping his brow and smiling at his cousin.

"I can see that." Greg hesitated. "Do me a favor?"

"Sure. What?"

"Don't offer one of them to Maya Logan."

"I hadn't intended to." Michael's brow knit. "Isn't she living in your extra apartment?"

"Yes. She is."

The pastor began to grin. "Ah, I see. You want her to stay there and you're afraid she might choose to move out here if I gave her the option."

"Something like that."

"Can I assume your intentions are honorable, cousin?"

That made Greg blush and stare at the younger man. "You sound like her father."

Michael laughed. "I am, in a way. My job makes me father, brother, friend, teacher and confessor, sometimes all at the same time." He sobered. "You haven't answered my question."

"I'd never do anything to hurt Maya, if that's what you're asking."

"Maybe not physically. I'm talking about breaking her heart. Are you sure you won't do that?"

Greg had no ready answer for him. If his own feelings were any indication, there was more than *one* heart on the line, and he had no idea what he was going to do about it.

Maybe the kindest, smartest thing he could do was stay away from her. It wouldn't be easy but he supposed it was worth a try. Then, if they were still attracted to each other later, he'd ask her for a real date.

What if she turns me down flat?

Then he'd know for sure, wouldn't he? That hit him so hard it hurt.

Chapter Twelve

Looking back, Maya couldn't believe all that had happened in the few weeks since the disaster. Tommy had started spending all his spare time hanging around either the church or the Garrison building and had begun running a few simple errands for them, swelling with pride when Greg had insisted on paying him for doing so.

The makeshift memorial for Marie had grown so big Jesse had had to ask folks to stop contributing to it but Maya could tell he'd been touched by everyone's heartfelt participation just the same. The only element that had still not been resolved was her family's missing heirloom engagement ring. Jesse had found everything else in the rubble of his kitchen except that one ring that mattered most.

She would have preferred if Clay had contacted her directly, but apparently he hadn't gotten her new phone number and called the Circle L and had spoken with Jesse. Sadly, Clay had made no mention about when he might be coming home to Kansas, much to Maya's dismay and disappointment.

She and Greg had settled into a routine, working together amicably during the day, then parting in the evenings. It was hard for her to keep from walking down the long hall and knocking on his door to borrow the proverbial cup of sugar but she managed to restrain herself. Layla, however, had no such reservations and spent as much time dropping in on Greg as she did staying at home. The child was clearly smitten with the man. Unfortunately, so was her mother.

Grumbling to herself—about herself— Maya found she could only tidy up the apartment so many times on the weekends before she grew too restless to remain inside. She was still waiting for the final insurance inspection and report on her damaged house so she didn't dare begin rebuilding, nor could she do much cleanup of the site without risking losing some of the settlement money.

Therefore, she had dropped Layla at day care and headed for the church basement to see if there was any task that needed doing.

To her dismay, Greg was there, too. He'd been instrumental in setting up a lost and found, complete with a computerized listing of the items that had been turned in, and was bringing those files up to date while showing Tommy Jacobs how to use a computer.

Greg grinned the minute he looked up from the keyboard and spotted her. "Hi." Leaning to one side to peer around Tommy and the monitor he asked, "Where's the princess?"

"With Josie in day care. She needs the extra money and I need a break."

"You know I'd be glad to babysit any time you want."

"Layla spends too much time at your place as it is. She must drive you crazy."

"Not at all. She's full of questions so she keeps me entertained." He ruffled the boy's hair. "So does this guy. I'm teaching them how to paddle a kayak."

"In the living room?"

"For now. Layla will have to be a lot older to do it for real. If I had one that held two people, maybe I could take turns giving the kids a chance to…"

"No," Maya said flatly. "Absolutely not. You are not taking my child out in a tiny little boat like that and that's final."

"I'll go!" Tommy piped up.

Laughing, Greg said, "Not for a while, okay?"

He went back to working on the computer and started typing while Tommy rolled his eyes, made a disgusted face and chose to make himself scarce.

Curious, Maya approached. "Have you had any word on that antique ring Jesse couldn't find? I know it's a minor thing compared to all the losses that other folks have reported but it's important to my family history."

"There was a small gold and diamond ring turned in. Here. Let me pull it up." He hit a few keys and a digital image appeared. "Is this it?"

Maya shook her head. "No. It's close, though. The ring Jesse gave Marie is unique. I'm positive that's not it. I can't understand how it got separated from her wedding band and letter. They were all together before the tornado struck the house."

"I'm surprised he found any of that stuff, considering."

"Me, too. It originally was our great-great-many-times-removed-grandmother Emmeline's, back in 1860."

Maya had started to turn away when Greg said, "Speaking of losses, have you heard anything about your insurance claim?"

"No, why?"

He shrugged. "Just wondered. I happened to be driving down Logan Street the other day and there were men with cameras and measuring tapes going over your house inch by inch. I questioned them to be sure they were legit and they said they were the ones who'll be making the official structural report."

"And you didn't tell me?"

"I figured you knew."

"No. Did they say how much longer it would take?"

"I didn't ask that. In view of their work-load, I suppose there's no hurrying them."

She sighed deeply and perched a hip on the far edge of the desk where he was working. "I suppose not. I'd just really love to be back in my own house." Seeing his crestfallen expression she was quick to add, "I like the apartment. Really I do. It's just that Layla needs a yard to play in and I want to feel at home."

"I understand."

"Do you? That place isn't just a plain house to me. I bought it with my share of my parents' estate, after Jesse bought out my third interest in the Circle L. I've always felt as if it was their gift to me. That probably sounds silly."

"It's not silly at all. Remember, my offer to help you make the repairs still stands."

"It does?"

Greg began to frown. Getting to his feet he circled the desk and stopped close to Maya. "Of course it does. Haven't you learned by now that my word is as good as any written contract?"

"I just thought...I mean..."

"I know exactly what you mean, Maya." He reached for her hand and clasped it gently. "You and I have both been pretty confused since the storm shook everything up."

"*I* sure have," she replied, permitting him to hold her hand, enjoying every second of that contact.

"I thought things might be moving too fast, at least they were for me, so I backed off to give you a chance to catch your breath."

"Of course." She wondered if he could tell that she was actually having trouble finding air just then. When Greg was this close, speaking this intimately, she felt as if she were floating, barely able to function. And certainly unable to force herself to put any distance between them.

"Let me help you with your house, the way we'd planned," Greg said with a pleading lilt. "We can work together, build something solid and lasting."

Maya wondered if he was still talking about lumber and plaster or if he might be referring to their relationship. Either way, she could not bring herself to rebuff him. One quick glance into his eyes and she was lost in the depths of his sincerity, his evident concern. And, if her imagination wasn't playing tricks on her, his affection.

"I'd like that," she said, surprised to hear her voice quaver.

"Good. You're not going to change your mind, are you?"

"Of course not. My word is every bit as good as yours."

"I'm certainly glad to hear that," Greg said as he smiled slightly and leaned closer.

Maya might have retreated if he had not still held her hand. She could feel his warm breath on her face, see the tenderness in his gaze.

She closed her eyes, lids fluttering. For a second she was afraid he might back away.

Then, his lips brushed hers for the briefest moment and she knew her imagination had not even come close to portraying the wonder and beauty of their first kiss.

Only the unexpected appearance of other parishioners, and a giggle from the ever-present Tommy Jacobs, kept her from throwing her arms around Greg's neck and asking for another.

Greg had loaned Maya his SUV a few times and didn't know she'd found herself another vehicle until she drove up to his father's estate while he was visiting there.

As she parked the compact maroon two-door in the semicircular drive that fronted the historic home and climbed out, her sunshine-yellow sundress and bright, joyful attitude reminded Greg of a Kansas spring morning.

He called a greeting from the porch. "Hi. Nice car. What brings you all the way out here? Were you trying out your new wheels?"

He watched her start up the limestone stairs that led from the drive to the first tier of lawn that had once been a formal garden. The spring-fed, decorative pond and fountain were now dry and grass had taken the place of the beautiful flowers his mother had always planted when she had been alive.

Maya was waving a handful of papers and grinning from ear to ear. "No. I was looking for you. I got the report and the insurance check. Already!"

"That's great. Was it satisfactory?"

"I think so. I have no idea what materials cost." She showed him the check. "Will this be enough?"

"Looks like it to me."

She beamed. "Great. When can we go to work?"

"Whenever you want," he answered, welcoming Maya onto the covered porch. "Would you like to come in?"

"I don't know that I should," Maya replied, seeming unusually reluctant. "Remember, your dad and mine never agreed on anything, especially about how to run the High Plains government, what little there is."

"That's all past history."

"For you and me, maybe. Funny how things worked out, isn't it? Our parents were political rivals not a bit friendly to each other, yet we do fine."

He clasped her hand and was thrilled when she wove her fingers between his. "We do, don't we? Where's the princess this morning?"

"Vacation Bible School. Last time I saw

her she was busy trying to explain the finer points of Christianity to Tommy—*and* to her teachers."

"That must have been entertaining to watch."

Maya grinned. "Actually, I had trouble keeping a straight face. Then, when I stopped to pick up my mail and saw this settlement, I decided to come find you so we could celebrate together."

"I'm glad you did."

Greg was about to escort her around to the side of the house and show her a garden bench and trellis he'd just restored when the mahogany front door swung open and his father stepped outside. One look at the old man's expression told Greg far more about Dan's foul mood than he wanted to know.

"What's she doing here?" Dan demanded.

"You remember Maya Logan, don't you, Dad? She came looking for me."

"Figures. She sure as blazes didn't come to visit me." He was wheezing as he spoke. "Doesn't belong here, anyway." Glaring at Greg, he added, "You should know better than to get involved with the likes of her. She tell you she's got a kid and no sign of a husband?"

Positioning himself between Maya and his father, Greg said firmly, "That's enough."

"Oh, so that's how it is, eh? Fine. Hang out with riffraff if it makes you happy. I can always cut you out of my will."

"And leave all this to who?" Greg asked, gesturing at the three-story limestone mansion with its red metal mansard roof and vast array of outbuildings to match. He was so angry he was trembling. "You know what? I don't care what you do. Sell everything and burn the money you get, for all I care."

"Hah! You can't fool me. You came back here to kiss up to me so you'd be sure I didn't leave my estate to somebody else."

"No," Greg countered, standing stiffly to face the man he had once idolized, then come to despise. "I'm here because Michael told me how sick you were. I thought maybe you and I could finally make peace."

"You never were worth a lick after your mama died," Dan shouted, beginning to cough. As soon as he regained control and caught his breath he added, "I see you didn't learn a thing in those fancy schools I sent you to."

Slipping his arm around Maya's shoulders Greg started to guide her away, to take her far from the vitriol his father was spewing. He could take that kind of harshness. He was used to it. But there was no excuse for Dan's treatment of Maya.

All Greg said to her was, "I'm sorry."

When she pulled away, she paused and gazed up at him to reply, "No. I'm the one who should be apologizing. I never should have come here."

Clearly, she had been badly hurt by the old man's words. It felt as if all the progress they had made in their budding relationship during the past few weeks had vanished in moments. Moments there was no way to erase.

How many others felt the same horrible way about her and Layla? Maya wondered, pacing her apartment. How many were too polite or too Christian to say exactly what Dan Garrison had? Did she dare think there might be many? Was that fair, or was she borrowing trouble? Perhaps both.

She wanted to unburden herself to Reverend Michael but couldn't bring herself to do so. Not now. Not yet. If he looked at her the way Greg's father had, she didn't think she could take that rejection.

Nevertheless, the urge to act, to do something to mend Greg's rift with his father, was strong within her. Should she go back to the Garrison estate, face the old man and try to explain? Did she have enough courage? An even better question was, would Dan listen to her?

So what if he didn't? she reasoned, angry with herself for hesitating. "If God be with me, who can stand against me?" she paraphrased, hoping scripture would bolster her flagging resolve. It did. Some. So did constant, beseeching prayer. Finally, she came to the conclusion that nothing she might say or do could make things worse between Greg and his father than they already were, so what was she waiting for?

Out of plausible excuses and trembling at

the thought of once again facing Dan Garrison, Maya climbed back into her car and headed toward the estate. She didn't know what she was going to say. She simply knew she must try. Dan was probably about to meet his Maker. Facing that final judgment with a heart full of unresolved anger and resentment was the worst thing imaginable.

As she drove she tried rehearsing a plausible speech. It was hopeless. No sooner had she had a valid thought than it was replaced by confusion. By the time she once again stopped in the estate drive, she was so befuddled she hardly knew her own name.

"Thank You, Jesus. Greg has left," she whispered, noting that his SUV was no longer parked next to the house. It looked as if she'd have Dan all to herself, like it or not.

That idea proved wrong when she rang the bell and a nurse in a white uniform opened the door. "Yes?"

"I'm Maya Logan," she explained. "I was here earlier and I wondered if I might speak with Mr. Garrison again."

The young woman arched an eyebrow.

"Are you sure you want to do that? He's not in the best mood today."

"When is he?" Maya asked with a wan smile. "I'll take my chances. I shouldn't be long."

The nurse stepped back. "Okay. It's your funeral."

Following the nurse up the spiral staircase to the second floor, Maya managed to swallow past the lump in her throat. "Speaking of funerals, what is his current condition? I wouldn't want to say anything that might make him worse."

"Hah! That old stinker will probably outlive us all. He likes to pretend he's on his last legs but I've worked for him long enough to know he's not as sick as he wants everyone to believe."

"He's faking?" Maya was astounded.

"Oh no, he has a chronic cough and emphysema, all right. But it's not immediately life-threatening." She lowered her voice. "If you want to know the truth, I think he convinced everybody he was at death's door just to get his son to come home to see him."

Maya sent up another silent prayer, this

time in thanks for what she'd just learned. *Okay, Father,* she prayed, *I know I won't kill him if I confront him. Now all I need is the strength to actually do it.*

If her hands hadn't been perspiring and her knees hadn't been shaking, she might have felt a lot more confident.

Remember, this is for Greg's sake, she told herself, knowing that was the truth. The man she was about to face was his father. That, alone, made him important.

The nurse knocked on a closed door, opened it in response to Dan's summons, and stepped out of the way.

Chin up, spine straight, shoulders back, Maya gathered her courage and entered the lion's den.

Greg had driven around the perimeter of the estate to check the fences and was in the barn, talking to the estate caretaker about needed repairs, when he heard a car door slam.

The nurse has probably quit, he thought, wondering how the poor woman had coped with his father for as long as she had. Most of the staff, or what was left of it, did as they thought best in spite of Dan's ranting and raving. If they hadn't, Greg knew the mansion and estate grounds would have fallen into ruin long ago. He wasn't sure whether the problem was that Dan didn't really care, or that he was so ill he was unaware of what needed to be done. Either way, it was the seasoned employees who had taken matters into their own hands and had managed to hold the place together.

Circling the house, Greg did not expect to see a car he recognized. *Maya?* What was she doing back here? He broke into a jog. The car was empty but the hood was still warm when he put his hand on it.

His head snapped around. He squinted at the house. *No. She didn't. She couldn't have. Dear God, please don't let her be inside. Not with him.*

Greg took the stone steps two at a time and burst in the front door. It took a few seconds for his eyes to adjust to the dimmer light of the foyer. There wasn't a soul in sight. Not Maya. Not the nurse. And not Dan.

He thought about calling out, then decided

against it. If Maya was there and Dan wasn't aware of it, the best thing to do would be to rescue her and usher her out before the old man had another chance to berate her.

Greg gritted his teeth as he hurried through the empty lower rooms and circled back to where he'd started. He looked at the stairway. His heart was in his throat and his pulse was pounding. If Maya was upstairs there was no telling how bad things would be. Or how long, if ever, it would take him to undo the damage his reprehensible, bitter father might do.

"I have nothing to say to you," Dan told Maya as he lounged against a stack of pillows at the head of a grand four-poster bed. "Go away."

She stood firm. "I came here to say my piece and I'm going to say it, whether you like it or not."

He laid his hand on his chest. "I'm a sick man. I can't take stress."

"No, but you sure can hand it out, can't you?" Sensing that she had surprised him by her candor she edged closer. Apparently, so few people stood up to Mr. Garrison he didn't know how to react when someone did.

"I spoke the truth about you."

"With malice," Maya said, nodding. "But, yes, you were right. I am an unwed mother. I love my little girl and no matter what you or anyone else says, I'm proud of her. Proud to be her mother."

"Hah!"

"I don't care if you choose to believe me or not," she said flatly. "That's not what's important. I came here to talk to you about your son."

"Gregory is no concern of yours."

"Maybe that's true. But he is a concern of yours, isn't he? That's why you decided to make the most of your condition. You wanted him to come see you."

"He should be here. I'm dying."

"We all are, little by little," Maya said. "If this were your last breath, would you want to go when you haven't made peace with your only son yet?"

The old man's jaw dropped. He stared at her.

"Are you afraid to love and lose him the way you lost his mother?" She could see that her assumption was close to the truth. Tears had begun to glisten in Dan's rheumy eyes.

"That's none of your business."

"You're right, it isn't. But what if you miss out because you were too stubborn to give a little, to get to know the fine man your son has become?"

The tears that had been pooling in his eyes began to slide down his cheeks. Moved, Maya stepped closer and took one of his hands. "I don't pretend to have all the answers. I just know that you've been pushing Greg away for a long, long time. Don't you think it's time you stopped?"

All Dan said was, "Get out of here. Leave me alone."

Any conviction that Maya had had that she was on a God-given mission to bring reconciliation abruptly left her. It was obviously time to step back. To stop trying to convince him and to leave before she said too much and ruined all the good she may have done up to that point.

What she wanted to do, in her own strength, was continue to reason with Dan and stay until he finally came to his senses.

It didn't take a genius to realize that that would be the wrong approach. If he was half as stubborn as Greg was, any further discussion would make matters worse, not better.

Disappointed that things had not worked out exactly as she had envisioned, Maya released the old man's hand and backed toward the door.

She was thankful she'd mustered the courage to visit him and speak her mind. And she was glad she'd been able to find words that had seemed right.

Now, however, all she wanted to do was make a dash for her car and escape from the Garrison estate as fast as possible.

Chapter Thirteen

Greg encountered Maya halfway up the spiral staircase. She wasn't weeping, as he'd feared, but she didn't look happy as she tried to sidle past, either.

He reached for her. She shook her head and dodged, then ran the rest of the way down the stairs and burst out the door.

Wondering if he should follow or go find out what his father had said to her this time, Greg decided it would be best if Maya had a little time to cool off before he tried to reason with her. He couldn't imagine how Dan could have treated her any worse than he already had. Then again, his father had never been known for diplomacy.

When he entered the older man's suite, however, he was astounded to see that Dan was clearly moved to tears. Surprised, Greg stood there and stared.

"Well, what are you looking at?" his father asked before blowing his nose. "Haven't you ever seen an allergy attack before?"

"You didn't take your medicine this morning?"

"Yeah. That's it. Forgot the pills."

"What did you say to Maya Logan?"

"Nothing. I just told her to go away. I hope she had the good sense to do it."

"She did." Greg gritted his teeth. "We may as well get this out in the open, Dad. I'm not sure if Maya will have me after all the awful things you've said to her, but I love her and I'm planning to ask her to marry me."

"You're a fool if you do."

"Am I? Seems to me I remember a story about Grandfather telling Mom the same kind of thing about you. Was that a mistake?"

To his amazement, the older man's tears resumed. Worried, Greg approached the bed. "Are you all right?"

"No. Yes." He cursed under his breath. "I don't know."

"Are you having difficulty breathing?"

Dan made a sour face and shook his head slowly. "No, son. My breathing is not a whole lot worse now than it was years ago. I just…" He hesitated, swallowed hard. "I just wanted you to come home."

"What?"

"You heard me. I'm not getting any younger and, as your girlfriend reminded me, I may be meeting my Maker before much longer. I—I wanted to see you again. To get to know the man you'd become since your mother died."

"You sent me away," Greg said, puzzled.

"Yes. I did. You reminded me too much of her, I guess. She'd always been closer to you than she was to me."

"Maybe that was because you berated her for every little thing she did wrong. And even for some things that were right."

"That was just my nature. Your mother knew that when she married me."

"And she loved you deeply, in spite of everything," Greg told him.

That statement was enough to bring quiet sobs from Dan. Greg placed a steadying hand on his father's thin shoulder and waited until he had regained a bit of composure before asking, "Do you want me to go, or stay with you for a little while?"

"I think I'd just like to be alone and think things over," Dan said haltingly. "I'll be fine."

"You're sure?"

"As sure as I ever am," the older man replied. "When you see that Logan girl, tell…tell her I'm sorry."

Maya had figured it was best to physically work off some of her excess energy and frustration, so she'd left Layla playing happily in preschool later that afternoon, changed into work clothes and headed for her home on Logan Street. The city had arranged to have extra refuse picked up at the curb until the tornado damage had all been removed, and it was a real relief to finally be able to start straightening up the place.

She pulled on heavy gloves, then started her own pile of branches and broken boards, taking care to keep from stirring up the bits of fiberglass insulation, although most of it had been blown away during the original storm.

Many of her neighbors had already either received their insurance settlements or had proceeded without them. Her house was one of the last waiting for cleanup and rebuilding. It was also one of the only ones badly damaged in that section of the residential district.

As Maya worked she thought about her meeting with Greg's father. Dan hadn't instantly become a loving father, as she'd hoped he might, but that kind of change wasn't within her control. She had merely presented an idea of how he might find the peace that had eluded him for so long. Now, it was up to him.

She paused in her work and removed her work gloves as Greg's SUV pulled into her driveway.

When he got out and came toward her he looked so serious she was afraid she might actually have caused his father's condition to worsen, in spite of the nurse's assurances that Dan wasn't that ill.

Her pulse pounded in her temples. "Is your father all right?"

"In a manner of speaking," Greg answered. "Care to tell me what you said to him?"

"Beats me. I was so nervous I can only remember bits and pieces of it. I'm sure I babbled something awful."

"Well, whatever you said it touched him." Greg stepped closer and took her hands. "He told me to tell you he's sorry."

The ecstatic grin on Greg's face warmed her soul. Maya smiled broadly in response. Her eyes grew misty. "What did he say exactly?"

"That he'd exaggerated about being at death's door to get me to come home. He actually admitted he wanted to get to know me better."

"That's wonderful." She meant that from her deepest heart, yet still yearned to hear that Greg's father had voiced forgiveness for his remarks about her having had Layla out of wedlock. When that wasn't forthcoming, she was positive he had not done so.

Hiding her disappointment she eased her

hands free from Greg's grasp, picked up her gloves and slipped them on again. "So, want to help me drag the rest of this stuff to the curb? There's supposed to be another special trash pickup Monday and I want to take advantage of it."

"Sure. Stand back. Let me do the heavy work."

"I've managed fine so far," she countered, more upset with herself for being hurt by the truth than she was at him for being bossy.

Although Greg paused for an instant after she spoke, he didn't reply directly. Instead, he went to work beside her as if they had always been a capable team.

"I'll figure out a lumber list and have the materials delivered ASAP," he said as they labored. "The best place to drop the load will be in the driveway so don't leave your car parked in the garage or you won't be able to get it out."

"Right. I understand." She was watching him. Waiting until he turned to face her and she could read his expression she asked, "Are you still planning to help me do the work or should I try to hire someone else?"

"Of course I plan to help you. I'll bring a couple of men with me for the rafter and roofing work so we have enough hands to do the job safely. The rest, I think you and I can handle by ourselves. You do know how to swing a hammer, don't you?"

"Of course. I used to help Dad at the ranch all the time. I can mend fences and build corrals with the best of them."

"That's what I figured. You'll feel more in charge if you work on your house, too. I'm looking forward to getting out from behind my desk again and using my muscles. The cleanup work on the Waters cottages was the most fun I've had in ages."

Maya flinched. She'd already had enough chances to look at his muscles, thank you. Even when he was wearing a suit she could tell what great physical shape he was in. That kind of unacceptable admiration had become so second nature she hardly realized she was doing it.

Which was one more good reason to hurry and repair her home, she told herself. The sooner she got away from Greg, the better. The minute the house was finished and she had paid him for the materials, she was going to start looking for another job. Working beside him, seeing him every day and not throwing herself into his arms like a lovesick fool, was the hardest challenge she had ever faced.

She cast a sidelong glance at him and her heart raced. He was so dear, so sweet. *So unsuited for her,* she added ruefully. Dan's words had been crude but his opinion was valid. She had made a terrible mistake and she was still paying for it. She always would be, in some respects.

Yes, God had forgiven her. That wasn't the same as being free of the consequences of her sins. Those remained in the form of the dearest little girl Maya had ever known.

If keeping and loving and raising Layla by herself meant she would never be considered good enough for a man like Greg Garrison, then so be it.

Greg had checked often at Lexi's veterinary hospital and the animal shelter, and had also kept in touch with the older woman who had collected frightened pets immediately after the tornado. Sadly, there had been no sign of Tommy Jacobs's missing dog, Charlie.

Greg had encountered the boy often and when he spotted him wandering around in the park, he hailed him. "Tommy! Hi. How's it going?"

The boy didn't answer. That didn't deter Greg. He joined him and they sat on the grass near the river in companionable silence for a few minutes before Greg tried again.

"I keep hoping Charlie will show up," Greg said with a sigh. "Have you heard anything?"

Tommy shook his head and stared at the placidly flowing water. Enough trash had been cleaned up that it had almost been restored to its original beauty and the bridge was once again open, but it was clear that the child wasn't really observing any of those details.

"I think we should put a lost-and-found ad in some newspapers so we get the word about Charlie to places that are farther away," Greg said. "What do you think?"

The boy's head snapped around. His blue

eyes were wide. "I don't know how to do that."

"I do. And I know what Charlie looked like so I can describe him. Do you happen to have a picture we could use, too?"

"No." Tommy's lower lip began to quiver with emotion. "I can remember how he looked without any dumb old picture. I'll never forget him."

"I'm sure you won't. Say, how about rescuing another pup in the meantime? I know you've seen lots of homeless dogs at the animal shelter. Then Charlie would have a buddy to play with when he gets home."

"I don't want a different dog. I want Charlie." Tommy continued to pout. "Besides, Mrs. Otis wouldn't let me have another one."

"Why not? Is she still sick?"

"Yeah. I can tell Mr. Otis is real worried."

This was not the first time the boy had mentioned that things had not returned to normal at the Otis home since the tornado. "What's the matter with her? Do you know?"

"Nope. They don't tell me stuff like that.

But I listen to them talking when I'm supposed to be asleep. They said…" His voice cracked. "They said I might have to go away to another foster home. Then I'd *never* find Charlie." With that, he began to sob.

Greg put his arm around the boy's shoulders. He wanted to do something for him. But what? He wasn't familiar with the workings of the foster-care system in Kansas so he had no idea what the child might be facing. That was the first order of business, he decided. He'd look into it and see if there was some way to intercede, to let the child remain in High Plains. Surely someone would take him in. Maybe Nicki Appleton had room for another child.

The idea that the person to volunteer should be *him* hit Greg like a punch in the stomach. No way. He wasn't father material. He had a business to run and too many other concerns. Besides, didn't a kid need two parents?

Those mental ramblings carried his mind immediately to Maya, as did most other thoughts of late. What a great family they would make: him, Maya, Layla…and Tommy. The idea made him smile. It was farfetched, of course, yet it refused to go away even when he rejected it outright.

He got to his feet and held out his hand to the boy. "Come on. Let's go grab an ice cream and then hit the computer at my office to place those ads. You can help me decide what to say. I'll even let you type some of the words if you want to, just like we practiced in the church basement."

The small hand that slipped into his and held tight touched his heart. This boy was as like him as any birth son could have been. Greg knew exactly what it felt like to be alone, rejected, in search of a place that felt secure. He and Tommy were kindred souls. He accepted that without question.

The dilemma then became, what was he going to do about it?

Maya was working at Garrison Investments when Greg and Tommy arrived. She greeted them both pleasantly while remaining busy at her own desk.

Out of the corner of her eye she could see what Greg was doing and it touched her deeply. It had been weeks since Charlie had run away in panic. Each day that passed meant a slimmer chance of his ever being recovered. And yet, Greg was keeping his promise to a six-year-old as if it were as important as a corporate merger.

Her fingers stilled over the keyboard. She listened. They were constructing a lost-and-found ad for Charlie, and from the sound of it, it was going to be a doozy, complete with a hefty monetary reward.

"I don't have any money," Tommy reminded Greg. "I bought ice cream and stuff with the quarters you gave me for bringing you stuff from the store."

"That's okay, son. I'll have plenty more errands you can run. Besides, I'll take care of the reward."

"Thanks."

Maya saw the kind, empathetic smile Greg gave the little boy and it brought unshed tears to her eyes. How could so many people believe that that man was anything but tender and compassionate?

It doesn't matter, she told herself. *Whatever Greg is or is not has no bearing on my life. It never will.*

That conclusion was so disheartening she nearly wept. Their work on her house would be finished soon, except for some interior painting, which she could do alone.

And then it would be time to pay Greg for the supplies he'd ordered and take her leave. Where she would find future employment was another question, one she had been mulling over for some time. There were few jobs in High Plains that paid as well as the one she currently had, but if she couldn't find a position around there, she could always consider driving to Manhattan to work. That trip didn't seem nearly as long and arduous now that she'd been making it regularly to visit Jesse's triplets in the hospital. Such a daily commute was doable, especially once Layla was in school all day.

That won't be for two more years, Maya reminded herself. *How are you going to cope with being near Greg for that much longer? You're already so in love with him you can hardly concentrate on your work, and when he's present in the office it's almost impossible.*

Boy, was *that* the truth. Maya chanced a

sidelong peek at him and found him staring back at her.

"Finish up whatever you're doing," Greg said soberly. "I have another job for you."

"Sure. What?"

"Just one second. We're almost done here."

Patiently, kindly, he encouraged Tommy to contribute to the text of the newspaper ads, then used a credit card to pay for them.

"Okay. That should do it," Greg said, getting up and escorting the boy to the door. "I'll let you know when we get any responses. In the meantime, I want you to go straight home and be really good for Mr. and Mrs. Otis. Understand?"

Wide-eyed, the child looked up at Greg as if he were seeing a superhero. "Uh-huh. Thanks, Mr. Garrison."

"You're welcome, Tommy. I was glad to be able to help."

The boy started to leave, then suddenly dashed back, wrapped his thin arms around Greg and gave him a hug.

In response, Greg ruffled Tommy's hair, patted him on the back and sent him on his way. When he turned back to Maya, she saw that his eyes were misty.

"I want you to research the foster-care system for Kansas," Greg told her. "I need to find out what qualifications are necessary to become a foster parent."

She was thunderstruck. "You *what?* Why?"

"Because Tommy may need a new place to live soon."

"Really? Why?"

Greg approached Maya's desk and casually perched a hip on its edge. "He says Mrs. Otis is having more heart problems and he thinks he might have to move again. I figured, if it wasn't too complicated, I might keep him for a while. You know, just till he finds his dog or gets over the loss."

"You'd do that? For him?"

"Of course I would."

When Greg reached out and gently patted her hand, Maya froze, barely breathing. They hadn't talked about anything personal in ages and she had wondered if he was ever going to discuss her so-called sins. This might be the opening she had been waiting for.

"I think that's wonderful of you," she said.

"Tommy can't help the situation he's in any more than my Layla can help being father-less. It's not her fault."

"I never said it was."

"I know. But your dad…"

"Apologized. I told you that."

Swiveling her desk chair, she stared at him, incredulous. "No, you didn't. You said he was sorry for being so outspoken. You never said he accepted me."

"He doesn't have to," Greg answered. "I do."

"You do? But I thought…"

"That your past bothered me? It does. It's a good thing you never told me the name of the lowlife who deserted you because if I got a chance to face him, I'd probably be tempted to deck him."

A lopsided smile began to lift one corner of his mouth. "However, in retrospect, I can see that we both owe the guy a lot. If he'd hung around longer, Layla might not need a daddy."

Maya was speechless as Greg circled the desk, gently clasped both her hands and urged her to her feet.

"She does, you know."

"Does what?" Maya managed to squeak out.

"Need a father. I was going to wait a little longer to bring this up but since we're already on the subject, I'd like to apply for that job." His grip on her fingers tightened. "If you'll have me."

"*Have* you?" Was he serious? Was he asking what she thought he was? Was it possible that all her wildest dreams were coming true? Or was her imagination tricking her with what she'd yearned to hear?

"I can see you're not totally convinced," Greg said, sobering but continuing to hold her hands. "That's okay. Give it some time. Talk to Michael if you think it will help. Once you're back in your own home it should be easier for me."

"Easier?" She knew she was starting to sound like a half-witted parrot but she was barely able to speak at all, let alone form sensible replies.

"Yes. Easier. I'm tired of pacing the floor and lecturing myself about not going down the hall to see you when that's all I can think about."

"It is?" Maya was positive that her blossoming grin was silly-looking because it was stretched so wide it hurt her cheeks.

"As if you didn't know."

"I didn't." The tenderness and sincerity in his eyes helped her finally find her voice. "I really and truly didn't."

She sighed deeply, tellingly, before continuing, "All of a sudden you stopped paying as much attention to me as you had been. I was sure you'd written me off after—after you'd found out I'd never been married."

"Because you fell in love with the wrong person when you were young and impressionable and trusted him too much? No, Maya. If anything, I admire you for staying single to take better care of your little girl. I'd like to help you do that from now on."

"You—you would?"

"Yes. I love you."

"I—I love you, too." Her voice was breathy, almost inaudible, though her heart wanted to shout it from the rooftops.

"Then marry me? Let me be Layla's daddy."

"You really want us both?"

"Of course I do."

A disturbing thought suddenly struck her. "What— what about Tommy?"

"I'd like to include him, too, if you wouldn't mind too much. If I qualify as a foster parent, that is."

"Mind? I'd love it. We could even adopt him!"

"Whoa. One thing at a time." Greg's smile had returned and he was gazing at her with adoration. "You have to accept my proposal before we consider adopting more kids. Can I take that as a yes?"

Standing on tiptoe she slipped her arms around Greg's neck and echoed his word, a single, sincere yes, just before she kissed him.

As he held her close and kissed her in return, she marveled at God's amazing gifts. He had given her more than the simple love she'd yearned for, prayed for. He had given her an entire family. Her life wasn't over because she'd defied society and had kept her darling Layla. It was just beginning. She could hardly wait.

Epilogue

Michael had acted thrilled when Greg had broken the news to him later, particularly because Greg had professed a return to his Christian faith at the same time.

"I wouldn't want to think you were saying this just for Maya's sake," the pastor remarked.

"I'm not. She played a part, of course, but I think I've wanted to *come home* for a long time."

Michael embraced him. "In that case, welcome back."

"Thanks. So, how's it going for you?" Greg asked as the cousins shared a late evening stroll along the banks of the river behind the church and parsonage.

"Fine. I may actually survive having a willful fourteen-year-old like Avery living under my roof. I know my sister misses her but we all agree that staying with me is the best way to get the kid straightened out."

"I wasn't exactly referring to your niece," Greg said. He watched Michael's dark eyebrows arch.

"Oh? Then what? Who?"

"Heather Waters. I heard she's coming back to town any day now." The astonishment on Michael's face made him chuckle. "What? You don't think I remember?"

"There's nothing to remember. Heather and I were just friends. There was nothing else between us."

"Only because she was going to marry your best buddy, not because you weren't madly in love with her, even after the wedding fell through," Greg said with a knowing smile.

"That was a long time ago. Situations change. People change."

"So, there's no soft spot in your heart for her now?"

Michael's deep breath and ensuing sigh was telling. "Not exactly."

* * * * *

Dear Reader,

As you have probably already discovered, this is book number one in a series of six. I wish I could have tied up all the loose ends for you, but if I had, there would have been no more secrets for the following five books and the other authors to reveal!

When I was asked to write about a tornado hitting a small town I had no idea how emotionally taxing it would be for me, living on the fringes of "Tornado Alley" myself and having experienced nearby twisters more than once.

Those of us who know what it's like to try to cope after such a storm want to offer special thanks and praise to the professional rescuers and the many hard-working volunteers who are always ready to pitch in and do whatever is necessary to help restore order and speed healing. You are truly God's heart and hands.

I love to hear from readers. The quickest replies are by e-mail:

Val@ValerieHansen.com

or check out my Web site:
        www.ValerieHansen.com.
By regular mail you can reach me at P.O.
Box 13, Glencoe, AR 72539.

Blessings,

Valerie Hansen

QUESTIONS FOR DISCUSSION

1. Have you ever lived in a small town like High Plains? If so, was it similar in the way the people related to each other? Why or why not?

2. Have you ever experienced being caught in a natural disaster? What was it? How did you cope?

3. Do you think it's normal for some people to react in totally opposite ways to losing possessions, or should they all be unhappy? Why might they not be?

4. If a Christian is trusting God, might he or she still question the results of the disaster? Do you think God gets angry if that happens?

5. Does it seem unfair that some residents had very little damage while others lost almost everything? Who is wise enough to decide? Are we?

6. When Maya and her daughter are reunited, Maya is joyous in spite of the destruction all around her. Why is that logical? Should she try to be more solemn or rejoice as her heart tells her to?

7. Greg steps up and offers help as best he can. Since he is more able to do so, isn't God expecting him to use his gifts for others?

8. What about the folks who lost almost everything? Do you think they still gave of whatever they had left? Would you be able to give to others if you'd lost everything? Why or why not?

9. High Plains Community Church treated everyone equally, whether they were church members or not. Is that biblical? When did Jesus do the same kind of thing?

10. Why do you think so many material possessions were unclaimed after the storm?

11. Tradition was important to the people of High Plains. As our cities have grown, we have lost some of that feeling of close community. Is there any way you and I can help restore it no matter where we live?

12. The committee to rebuild the old town hall is made up of volunteers, some of whom work harder than others. Is that bad? Suppose everyone didn't agree and nothing got done because of it?

13. Greg eventually comes to understand his taciturn father. Was Maya out of line by speaking so bluntly to the older man? Is "tough love" sometimes best? When would it be wrong? Why?

14. Maya is quick to fall in love with Greg. She does plan to get premarital counseling, but is it possible that she was still too influenced by the trauma of the tornado to be positive she's really in love? Have you ever been sure of

love, only to find that you were fooling yourself?

15. Only one love is guaranteed—God's love. Have you ever asked for and received it? If not, why not do so right now? It's not hard. All you have to do is open your heart to Jesus, ask to become one of God's children and He will bless you just as he has me.

*Turn the page for a sneak preview of
book two in the*
AFTER THE STORM *miniseries,*
MARRYING MINISTER RIGHT
*by Annie Jones,
available in August 2009
from Steeple Hill Books.*

"Hey, didn't you come from High Plains?"

"High Plains?" Heather stopped in her tracks as if the very name had thrown up a force field that she could not escape. That only added to her confusion as she shook her head and asked, "Why do you ask?"

Her assistant Mary Kate pointed to the TV hung in the lobby.

"An F3-level tornado devastated the small community of High Plains, Kansas, yesterday evening," the TV announcer was saying.

"What?" Heather stepped forward. She'd been so busy with work and her father she hadn't heard any news all day.

"The destruction is widespread," the announcer went on. "Emergency crews are on the scene. We are still waiting to see if there are any deaths or serious injuries."

Dead or injured? In High Plains? Heather staggered forward toward the small, flickering screen. A knot tightened in her stomach.

"You grew up there, right?" Her assistant looked from the broadcast to Heather, then back to the broadcast.

"Yes, it's…" A place she had not visited or even so much as driven through since she had left it behind a decade ago. Heather imagined rubble where once had stood homes and businesses. Perhaps here and there something would remain seemingly untouched.

To her surprise, an aching sense of the familiar washed over her. The threat of tears blurred her vision. "It's *home.*"

All her life that was all she had wanted. A real home. Her mother tried so hard to make one for their family but no amount of love and kindness on her part or striving for perfection on Heather's had made it happen. Nothing either of them did could make Heather's father love her.

"At present the town is using High Plains Community Church, which escaped virtually unscathed in the storm, as a base of operations."

The image of the simple old white church flashed on the screen and the world seemed to spin backward through time. Her cheeks flashed hot. Her knees wobbled for only a moment before she took a deep breath and shut her eyes to steady herself.

The day she'd left High Plains for good, never looking back, she was supposed to have been married in that very church. As long as she lived she would never forget opening the envelope in the sanctuary where she had spent so many joyous days of her life. In that envelope, delivered by a private investigator hired by her fiancé's family, she found a truth her mother had taken to her grave. Edward Waters was not her biological father.

And John Parker, son of the wealthiest family to ever live in High Plains, wanted nothing to do with her. There would be no marriage. For only a moment Heather had blamed the circumstances spelled out in the private investigator's report. But young though she was, she wasn't so foolish as to think in this day and age someone would refuse to marry a person because they didn't know their own father. No, Heather had been dealt two blows that day. She now understood why Edward Waters would never love her and that, despite his many youthful professions, that John Parker never really *had* loved her.

Her world had fallen apart that wretched day and she had crumbled with it.

She had come so far since then, yet this awful reminder of her hometown proved to her that she may have moved away but she had not wholly moved on.

"Built in 1859, the church remains much as it did then, a beacon to those in need." The reporter spoke with a cultivated calm that belied the tragedy of the situation. "We interviewed the minister from the church earlier today and here's what he had to say."

Heather raised her hand to block the screen from her view. "I'll look this up online later tonight. It's just horrible but…it really doesn't have anything to do with me anymore. It's not like I even know anyone there any—"

Just then, between her splayed fingers she caught a glimpse of a broad-shouldered man with wavy dark brown hair looking rumpled but in charge.

"Michael." Heather dropped her hand to her throat and fought to drag in a breath deep enough to allow her to speak above a dry, shocked whisper.

The image froze on the screen.

The years had treated him kindly. Given him fullness in the face and the beginning of lines fanning out from his startlingly blue eyes. Still, there was no mistaking him. "Michael Garrison."

"You know him?" Mary Kate's head whipped around.

The picture began to break up.

"I'm sorry." The news anchor came back. "We seem to have lost that connection. We'll go back to it after this message."

Heather exhaled slowly, her eyes on the TV where moments ago she had confronted her past. "Yeah, I know him. Or knew him. That is…I *thought* I knew him. The last time

I saw the man, I threw my wedding bouquet in his face."

"You were going to marry him?" Mary Kate stabbed her finger at the TV.

"No, he was just—" A friend? A friend would never have done what Michael Garrison had done. In many ways, his role in what happened that day had hurt Heather more than John calling the wedding off so cruelly. Because she knew why John couldn't go through with the marriage. Even though she still chafed at the way he had chosen to end their relationship, she had found a grudging respect for the fact that he hadn't gone forward with wedding vows he knew he could not honor for a lifetime. But Michael? What he had done? That, she could never understand. "Michael Garrison was just a—"

"Tell us, Reverend Garrison, what can people watching do to help?" The news correspondent had come back on. He thrust the mic into the bleary-eyed, disheveled minister's face.

Such a good face. Heather could still see the kindness and commitment in the way he stood firm among the chaos and destruction. In the fact that he looked as though he had not rested since the storm had hit. In the fact that he was willing to speak on behalf of those who could not at the moment speak for themselves, with no regard for his own needs.

"Reverend Garrison," she murmured, shaking her head. Michael had always talked about entering the ministry but she had never heard if he had followed through.

He stroked the stubby shadow of bristles along his jaw. When she had last seen him, he'd hardly been shaving at all. He had been so young then. They all had been.

"For the time being we have most of the basics covered," he said.

His hoarse voice tripped over her weary nerves the way she imagined a thumb would strum over the taut strings of a guitar, leaving them vibrating. The sudden clash of emotions the news churned up in her had left her feeling raw, she told herself. But deep down she knew something more was at play.

"This is not something that will be a quick

or easy fix." He shifted his weight. Tugged at his collar. Cleared his throat. All signs of his discomfort with this kind of media attention. Still, he clearly understood how important this moment was, the chance to get a message out, to speak for the people and the town he so loved. "We have a lot of damage, a lot we still don't know. We have a fund set up through a local bank for contributions. So anyone wants to help that way, we'd appreciate it."

"Done," Heather said softly even as Mary Kate lunged for a pen and paper to jot down the information scrolling across the bottom of the screen.

"And, of course, we could use your prayers," Michael concluded.

"Also done." Heather pressed her lips together, drew in a deep breath and finally looked away.

That was all she could do right now. Her father was ill; she couldn't leave town. Helping Hands Christian Charity was not designed nor was it equipped to rush in and give aid in situations like this. She had an obligation to the people who donated to the organization to adhere to their mission. Still, she would do all she could personally to help the town she still loved, even if it had not seemed to love her back.

"Is there anything else you'd like to say?" the reporter pressed on. "Anything more people can do to make a difference?"

For a second there was only silence.

Heather took the slip of paper from Mary Kate and did not look up. She did not need to see the man to know he was stroking his hand back through his hair, rubbing his chin and generally stalling for time. It was a habit he'd had since Little League. Always wanting to be sure he did and said the right thing, wanting to be conscious of other people's feelings. That was why, when he had totally ignored her feelings on the biggest day of her life, it had wounded her so deeply.

John had always called it being a big chicken. After Michael had let her put on her wedding dress and walk down the aisle only to be greeted by devastating news, Heather tended to agree with John's assessment.

She would send money to the town and

certainly pray for all of them but that was all she would do. All she *could* do. She turned away from the TV.

"There is one more thing," Michael finally spoke up. "There are some tourist cottages by the river, a whole row of them."

Heather tensed.

"I, uh, I used to know the owner," Mike went on. "Well, uh, the owner's daughter, actually."

A shiver went down her spine.

"These cottages survived in pretty good shape. They aren't luxury accommodations by any means, but for families who have nowhere else to turn, who want to stay in High Plains and be together, they could become a real, if temporary, home."

"Home," she whispered again. She spun around and searched first the background of High Plains behind Michael, then the man's face. He had practically just spelled out Heather's personal mission statement. She fought back the tears for the second time that night.

"If anyone knows how to get in touch with any member of the Waters family, or if any of them hear this interview… Heather, will you help us out if you can?" Michael finally asked outright.

"Is he talking to you?" Mary Kate's eyes grew wide.

"Yes." He was talking to her. As an old friend. As a man of God. Perhaps even as a nudge from God. "Mary Kate, make the call and tell Michael Garrison they can use the cottages. I'll get it cleared through my father."

"What if he asks to speak to you?" Mary Kate had already picked up the receiver, her hand hovering above the keypad on the phone.

"He had his chance to speak to me ten years ago and he kept quiet," she said softly.

"What? You really want me to tell him that?"

Heather blinked and came back to the present. "No. No, of course not. Tell him…" She looked out at her car next to Mary Kate's in the dark and otherwise empty parking lot. "Tell him I have a lot of personal and work-related issues colliding right now but I will come to High Plains as soon as I can, to do whatever I can."

Love Inspired®
SUSPENSE
RIVETING INSPIRATIONAL ROMANCE

These contemporary tales
of intrigue and romance
feature Christian characters
facing challenges to their faith...
and their lives!

**Four new Love Inspired Suspense titles are
available every month wherever books are
sold, including most bookstores, supermarkets,
drug stores and discount stores.**

Steeple
Hill®

Visit:
www.steeplehillbooks.com

Love Inspired.
HISTORICAL
INSPIRATIONAL HISTORICAL ROMANCE

Engaging stories of romance,
adventure and faith,
these novels are set in
various historical periods
from biblical times
to World War II.

NOW AVAILABLE!

Steeple
Hill®